D1625157

THE LAST OF THE JEDI

THE LAST OF THE JEDI

DEATH ON NABOO

Jude Watson

SCHOLASTIC INC.

New York   Toronto   London   Auckland   Sydney
Mexico City   New Delhi   Hong Kong   Buenos Aires

www.starwars.com
www.scholastic.com

ISBN-13: 978-0-439-68137-7
ISBN-10: 0-439-68137-5

Cover art by John Van Fleet

12 11 10 9 8 7   9 10 11/0

Printed in the U.S.A.
First printing, April 2006

STAR WARS

THE LAST OF THE JEDI

CHAPTER ONE

Meetings with the Emperor were always unnerving. Malorum just hoped this one wouldn't be fatal.

Malorum paused outside the airlock to the Emperor's private office, high on the top floors of the Senate office building. He had undergone the weapons scan. As the Emperor's most loyal subject, it was a process he found insulting, but he had to submit to it. Once he went through those doors, he'd be whisked in to see Palpatine by Sly Moore, that moonfaced nonentity who managed to slither herself into a position of power. *Probably by blackmailing the right beings*, Malorum thought, because he could find no other reason for her prominence. The usual jealous surge passed through him as he wondered, once again, why others got what he deserved.

He took a deep breath.

He needed a moment. He needed to remind

himself how well things were going. No matter what lies Darth Vader had told the Emperor, Malorum knew the truth. He was the best Inquisitor the Emperor had.

Ready now, Malorum strode through the door. He went through his usual battle of wills with Sly Moore. She glided her way toward him and he kept going to the door to Palpatine's inner office, so that it wouldn't appear that he was waiting for her to access it. He just walked right through — slightly ahead of her, of course.

He timed it perfectly.

His small victory died a quick death as Palpatine swiveled in his chair to face him. Right away, Malorum knew this was not going to be a good meeting.

He gathered his courage and walked forward into the grand red room. He loved this office. The bold red color, the bronzium statues of the Four Sages of Dwartii, the access to datafeeds that spewed out information constantly. You felt you were truly in the center of the galaxy, controlling everyone in it.

Palpatine stared at him with his pale eyes. Malorum wished, not for the first time, that Palpatine hadn't been so hideously scarred by the battle with Mace Windu. It was positively unnerving; you'd think that with all that access to the Force he could find a way to make himself look more attractive. When Malorum became Emperor (a thought Malorum only allowed to cross his mind occasionally; there was so much farther to go) he would make sure to get plenty of rest and a rejuvenating trip to the excellent surgeons of Belazura once a year.

"Why did you give an order to blow up the Jedi Temple?" The Emperor shot the question at him. So much for preliminaries.

"I was following through on an order by Lord Vader —"

"He said that you would claim that."

"But it's true." Technically. Vader had made the suggestion only to see how Malorum would react. Malorum had fallen right into his trap by protesting that he had files that would be destroyed. The next thing he knew, Vader was taking him to task for having secret files that weren't registered with the Inquisitors' main databank.

He had taken a gamble, attempting to blow up the Temple. He had actually enjoyed having his office there. To walk into that grand hallway was a thrill. It was visible evidence of the greatness vanquished by the power of the Empire. Proof that a Force connection wasn't enough; it was how you used the dark side of the Force that mattered.

He knew Emperor Palpatine was frustrated with the apprentice he'd ended up with. He had expected someone with awesome power, but instead he got a rebuilt body in a breath mask. Darth Vader was powerful, but compared to what he could have been . . . well, who wouldn't be disappointed?

What Palpatine needed was a new apprentice. Because of his Force-sensitivity, Malorum had been plucked out of obscurity. Palpatine had revealed that he was a Sith. He had explained what the Force was in detail and how, with training, Malorum could use it for great things.

Malorum had expected greater access because of that: dinners with the Emperor and his most trusted aides; confidences meant for him alone; invitations to Palpatine's private apartments in the exclusive 500 Republica residential tower. Instead, he himself was on the waiting list for an apartment, lined up with Senators and bureaucrats. It was infuriating!

Now he was scrambling to please Palpatine and being undercut by Darth Vader at every turn.

"You exceeded your authority," Palpatine went on. His gaze was as chilling as a monthlong vacation on Hoth.

Malorum looked to the bronzium statues for inspiration, then turned his gaze back quickly. He had learned to stand his ground with the Emperor. Never argue. Present your case, then change the subject if you can.

"The attack on Solace and her followers is proceeding," he said. He unfurled his best piece of information, the one he was holding in reserve like an expert sabacc player. "Everyone has been killed and the community destroyed. She is confirmed dead."

"And you saw this with your own eyes?"

"I received a report from the commander." Did the Emperor really expect him to travel all the way down to the Core, to the ancient ocean caverns?

"A Jedi is not dead until you see the body. Inform me when this is so."

He had been dismissed. Malorum made an instant decision to withhold the information that he had Ferus Olin in custody. He might need that at a future date. And he had plans for the former Jedi apprentice, plans that he was just beginning to form. Ferus was the only being he could find who could connect him to the old Darth Vader.

Malorum bowed and walked out, ignoring Sly Moore and proceeding directly to the express turbolift. As he descended into the Senate office building, he thought about what he knew . . . and what he still had to discover.

His most important piece of information was this: He knew that Darth Vader was Anakin Skywalker.

The Emperor didn't know that Malorum knew this. Before the tapes of the Temple attack had been erased, he had seen them. He hadn't been an Inquisitor then, just one of the trusted Imperial intelligence officers sent to the Temple after Order 66. He had seen what Anakin Skywalker had done. And he had seen the Jedi knight kneel down before the Emperor, who had called him "Darth Vader."

Since then he'd made it his business to discover everything he could about Skywalker. Bribes and surveillance and digging back into what had happened months before.

He knew that Anakin Skywalker had been a Jedi apprentice at the same time as Ferus Olin. He knew that Skywalker was the father of Senator Amidala's child, the child that had never been born. He suspected that the Senator had been treated on Polis Massa, but so far the disappearance of records had stopped the trail cold.

Secrets contained surprises. Once you knew a person's secrets, you had the key to destroying him.

Ferus Olin would be the key.

CHAPTER TWO

It wasn't so bad, for a prison. Ferus had seen worse.

He stirred on the hard duracrete where he slept . . . and found himself face-to-face with the biggest meer rat he'd ever seen, chewing on one of his boots.

Well. Maybe not.

He tossed his other boot at the rodent and it scurried away. He figured he might as well look the facts in the face. He'd landed in the worst prison in the galaxy, and unless someone near and dear to him — or even someone who didn't like him particularly much, like Jedi Master Solace — rescued him, he was stuck here, worked to death until he was executed.

It was the usual cunning plan of the Empire. Condemn the beings who displease you — don't bother with a trial, because your suspicions are enough — then stick them all in a stinking hole on a planet where nobody goes, force them to labor, don't even let them speak to one another, and then, when they're too weak to do you a bit of good, execute them. What a swell system to be stuck in. Trust him to find it.

So maybe breaking into the Temple wasn't the *best* idea he ever had. And then he had to go and do it twice. No wonder Malorum had been testy.

He had been looking for Jedi. Rumors had swirled that they were kept in a prison there. But the rumors were designed as a trick to lure any Jedi into a rescue attempt. Ferus had fallen right into the trap.

The need to find every last Jedi was leading him to places he'd never expected to go. Obi-Wan Kenobi, now in exile on Tatooine, had refused to become part of his plans for a secret base. Ferus didn't let that stop him. He knew there must be Jedi out there who had survived the purge. They needed a sanctuary. He had stumbled on a remote asteroid that constantly traveled the galaxy within a moving atmospheric storm. He had two trusted aides setting up a camp there, Raina and Toma, as well as the recovering Jedi Knight Garen Muln.

When he'd found Jedi Master Solace, he'd discovered that she'd set up a community next to the forgotten underground oceans of Coruscant. The raggedy society had built its homes on a series of catwalks over the sea in a vast cavern. When he'd told Solace what he'd seen in the Temple — a room full of lightsabers captured from murdered Jedi — she had been stricken by sadness and anger. Then he'd told her that he'd overheard that there was a spy in her camp, and she'd become enraged.

She'd talked him into breaking in again. He would need lightsabers, she argued, for the Jedi he was sure were out there. And she needed to discover the identity of her spy.

So they'd broken into the base of the Temple, thanks to Solace's odd ship with a mole miner aboard. But they'd run into too many stormtroopers and more trouble than they could handle. Now here he was, in prison, with an execution order just waiting to be carried out.

He was given a number when he arrived: 987323. He was told not to talk to any other prisoner and not to ask the guards for anything because he wouldn't get it anyway. "Not even for seconds on dessert?" he'd asked, and in response had received a force pike in the stomach. That had taken hours to recover from. He had to remember to keep his mouth shut.

The situation was hopeless, he supposed, but he had been trained as a Jedi, and so he resisted feeling hopeless. There was always a way. Or, as Yoda would say, *a way there always is.*

He wondered about Trever, the thirteen-year-old

who had pretty much adopted him as a guardian. He had been along to break into the Temple — both times. He didn't seem to want to leave Ferus's side. Would Solace take care of him? Not that Trever would let anyone take care of him, exactly. And not that Solace had the warmest of characters. Still, he hoped Trever was all right. He was a street thief and an explosives expert and a pain in the neck, but he was still a boy.

The rat returned, and Ferus winged his boot at it again. It retreated, baring its teeth in a rather human way that gave Ferus a chill. He hoped he wouldn't see those teeth sunk into his ankle later. Maybe sleeping wasn't such a good idea.

"Do you mind, chum?" The voice of his cellmate rose out of the corner. Ferus had been thrown into the cell in the pitch-black and hadn't met him yet. He was just a shape in the corner. "I'm trying to sleep."

"There's a meer rat —"

"You don't say. What a shock." Ferus could only see a gleam of pale skin across the space. "They like to eat boots. Use them as a pillow."

"Use my boots as a pillow?"

"What, duracrete is such a nice cushion? Keep a rock in your hand and crush its skull when you get a chance. Leave the body. The others will get the message. Better do it or else you'll find one chewing on your face in the middle of the night."

"I don't have a rock."

Ferus could hear his cellmate's sigh. "Why do I always get stuck with the new guy? Heads up." A good-sized rock suddenly loomed out of the darkness. Ferus caught it, but if he hadn't had quick reflexes it would have bashed in the side of his head.

"Thanks. So where am I?"

"Dontamo Prison. But don't worry, you won't be here long. One day soon you'll be dead."

"I got that impression. Has anyone ever escaped?"

"Death is your escape, my friend." Ferus heard his cellmate turn over to face him. Now he could see the gleam of his eyes. "All right, I can see that I won't get any sleep until I give you the lowdown. Whatever you do, don't get sick. No one who goes to the infirmary ever comes back. Second, don't talk to anyone during the day. And don't talk to me unless you have to. I have a whole fantasy world going on in my head, and I don't like to be interrupted. I'm on a picnic with my wife, and the sun is shining, and I'm about to eat one of her sweetberry tarts."

"You're married?"

"Never ask a personal question," the prisoner continued. "Never fall down. Never tell anyone you're innocent. Nobody had a trial here, so we've got the innocent and the guilty and it makes no difference. Nothing matters here except putting in your time until you get to die. Everybody fights over rations. That's the currency here. Eat fast. And one last thing, the most important thing — don't cross Prisoner 677780. He runs the gang here. We just call him 67. Don't even catch his eye. You'll be sorry if you do."

"Got it. Thanks."

"My advice is, think of the best day of your life and replay it in your head. Now leave me alone."

Ferus felt his cellmate turn away. He lay on his back, staring at the ceiling, and clutching the rock. Was this all he had left? Hanging on to a memory, replaying it until death came for him?

Best day of his life . . .

He and Roan, on a hiking trip on the neighboring world of Tati, deep in the forest, coming upon a waterfall that slid into a deep pool of green. They had been so hot, and they'd dived in, straight to the bottom. The water was so cold they came up shivering and laughing. . . .

He heard the rat scuttling forward and he brought his hand down, hard, with the rock in his fist. The rat lay still.

Those Jedi reaction skills sure could come in handy. . . .

CHAPTER THREE

Trever flattened himself on the metal walkway. He heard the ping of blaster fire and the cries from people being hit. He smelled smoke from the detonators and the burning dwellings. He heard the sound of bodies falling.

He was hiding, his usual position in a battle. But this time it was different. This time he couldn't move. His fingers shook as he curled them around the grating underneath him. His hiding place was good, behind one of the Imperial troops' own speeders. There was a guard, but he hadn't seen Trever. For a brief moment Trever had thought of stealing the speeder, but he knew he'd be blasted to bits in seconds.

When he and Solace had returned from the disaster at the Jedi Temple, Solace had heard the battle before he did. She had leaped off the ship and straight into the thick of it.

He had seen battles before, but none like this. He had run from Imperial officers, he had broken into buildings, he had taken the risks needed to maintain his own black-market operation, but this was different. This was terrifying. The eerily white stormtroopers were bent on annihilating everything in their path.

He had caught glimpses of Solace, fighting furiously to save her followers. He'd seen her moving, diving, never losing her balance or her grace despite the ferocity of her attack. Her lightsaber was a beacon of light, glowing green through the smoke.

She would lose. She would hold out as long as she could, but she could not win. There were simply too many of them. Almost everybody was dead now. Slaughtered without thought, without pause.

Rhya Taloon was dead. He saw her die. She'd been a Senator once, until they targeted her for prison or worse and she had joined the Erased, the group who'd destroyed their former identities and hid in the lower levels of Coruscant. She had fashioned a new, fierce look for herself, twisting her silver hair into horns and wearing holsters across her body. She'd learned how to shoot a blaster, but she'd never been very good at it.

He and Ferus had traveled down here with other members of the Erased, but now they were dead, too. It must be so, because all he could see were bodies. Among them lay Hume, who'd once been a pilot in the Republic Army. Gilly and Spence, the brothers who hardly spoke. Oryon, the fierce Bothan who'd been a spy for the Republic during the Clone Wars. Curran Caladian, the young Svivreni who'd once been a Senatorial aide, had leaped to defend the houses in the central catwalk. Trever had seen the stormtroopers send flame grenades into the homes and had turned away.

And Keets Freely, the journalist. Trever had seen his body, bloodied and battered, as he and Solace had run up to investigate. He couldn't believe it, couldn't believe that the mocking, indestructible Keets could fall. But fall he did, from a platform above, landing at Trever's feet. That had been the beginning of Trever's true terror.

In the short time he'd been traveling with them, they'd all become his friends. And now he didn't know what to do or where to go, because he was sure that this was the day he would die.

A new voice rose in his mind, not a voice of fear but impatience.

Well, if you're going to die, show some guts, will you?

He slowly, painstakingly, raised his head, ready for it to be blown off at any moment.

The battle had moved to an upper level of the catwalks and landings that twisted so crazily below the cavern walls. But there wasn't much battle left. He saw a few holdouts, but they were surrounded and soon would be dead. He wrenched his gaze away. He couldn't watch anymore, couldn't bear it anymore. . . .

Suddenly a streak through the smoke made him raise his head. Solace had made an incredible leap, jumping down from the topmost catwalk to the one just above Trever's head. Stormtroopers were pouring down the ramps after her. In another few moments they would corner her.

And he was here, hiding like a coward.

He had to help her, and do it fast. But how?

Stop hiding, Trever. That would be a start.

He snaked behind the other speeders and was able to get a better look above.

The stormtrooper guarding the speeders turned away from the noise of battle to take a communication — he could see him speaking into his helmet, straining to hear over the noise — and Trever leaped closer to the stairs that led to the next level. He landed behind a smoking heap of twisted metal that had once been a house. He slammed into a body and nearly levitated out of the space in terror until a strong hand clamped on his leg.

"Don't move."

It was Oryon, the Bothan. His face was blackened with smoke, his long mane a tangled mass. His tunic was torn and a long scratch ran down his upper arm. His eyes were reddened from the acrid smoke. He was the fiercest thing Trever had ever seen.

"Solace is —" Trever panted.

"I know. Do you have any charges left?"

Trever nodded, ashamed. He had been too afraid to set off many of his charges. He had hidden instead.

"I've got some grenades," Oryon said. "It might be enough."

"What are we going to do?"

"Blow the whole platform."

"But she'll fall."

"She's a Jedi. She'll survive. But they won't."

"Uh, and what about . . ." Trever gulped. "Us?"

"We'll do it from below, then get back to this platform."

Trever glanced down through the grate to the black sea below. *"Below?"* he squeaked.

"Are you ready?"

Ready? I'm ready to run the other way.

No — keep it together.

Trever nodded.

"Follow me."

Oryon took two strides and suddenly flipped himself over the catwalk railing. Trever moved cautiously forward and hung over the railing in astonishment. He saw that there were handholds and footholds below the grating, just random pieces of metal that you could hang on to in order to scrabble your way across, moving underneath the grating like a crab. Far, far below he saw the moving black sea.

There was nothing else to do but go over. A small part of him was pleased that Oryon was treating him as a comrade, assuming without question that he would do this. Ferus would have told him to continue hiding behind the speeder.

Trever swung one leg over, searching for a hold underneath. Then he slowly slid his hands down until his other toe found a hold.

They made their way upside down, looking up through the grating. Sometimes they had to curl their fingers through the grating itself to make progress. He just hoped that a stormtrooper didn't step on his fingers. Those boots looked pretty lethal. Trever knew his fingers would be raw after this, but strangely, the fear had left him and a grim determination to finish the job was pushing him forward.

When they were close, Oryon signaled him and spoke in his ear. "You have to go ahead. Set the timers for thirty seconds. That will give you enough time to get back. Then I'll throw the proton grenades from here. Set the charges carefully so only that catwalk blows."

Trever scrabbled forward, his fingers aching. He

would have to find a good place to anchor his feet and one hand while he reached into his utility belt. He made his way more quickly now, used to the feeling of being upside down. When he saw the white stormtrooper boots above, he set one charge, wedging it into the catwalk, then another and another, his biggest alpha charges. By the time he finished, his fingers were scraped raw.

Counting in his head, he went backward to where Oryon waited. "Five seconds," he grunted to the Bothan.

"Go," Oryon whispered.

Trever quickly scrabbled back in the direction he'd come. But he couldn't resist stopping to watch Oryon toss the grenades.

Oryon dropped one powerful arm and lobbed the grenade. It shot straight out then curled around the edge of the catwalk, sailing over the railing and onto the platform above. Without pausing, he threw the other three grenades.

Trever felt the explosion against his eardrums. Oryon was moving fast toward him, hand over hand. The catwalk had become a living thing, buckling and waving. It could break at any moment.

He risked another look back. The platform above was cracking, metal parting from metal with a groaning, scraping sound. The stormtroopers were starting to fall into one another as they desperately searched for traction. Some were trying to vault to safety to the catwalk or the platform below.

Solace was the only one who used the explosions to her advantage. She had ridden the blast like a wave and had shot into the air. Trever watched, breathless, as she somersaulted away from the stormtrooper army and fell — no, not fell, *soared,* completely in control — past the stormtroopers, over the groaning metal, over the heat, over the smoke, and down, down to the sea below.

"Hurry," Oryon urged Trever, his voice hoarse. "We've got trouble."

To Trever's horror, he saw that the catwalk was melting from the heat, shaking loose from the platform above. It must have been weakened from the battle's blaster fire. They couldn't make it to safety, he could see that. The catwalk began to fishtail as the platform above broke into pieces, sending stormtroopers sliding into the sea below.

"You've got to let go!" Oryon shouted. "We're not going to make it!"

"Let go? Are you nuts?" Trever felt his fingers cramp from trying to hold on to the twisting catwalk.

"It's the only way!" Oryon looked at him, his eyes intense. He suddenly flipped his legs forward and wrapped them around Trever's waist. Then he let go with one hand and pulled Trever against him. Trever felt the strength of Oryon's arms and legs, pure thick muscle. "I'll be with you."

Trever looked down. The sea looked black and dangerous. And very far away.

"I just want you to know something," he said to Oryon. "I can't swim!"

And then he let go.

CHAPTER FOUR

That brief conversation turned out to be one of the few Ferus had with his cellmate. Ferus knew his number — 934890 — but his cellmate never confided his name or anything else about himself. The only sentences he uttered were along the lines of "Move your boots."

Within a day Ferus became used to the routine, because he had to. Any hesitation about where to line up or what to do was met with a blow and a curse from the Imperial guards. He was a step ahead of the other new prisoners. His Jedi training had taught him how to anticipate, how to read body cues, how to, as the Jedi said, "See without looking." He was able to enter the flow of the prison without disturbance.

Also, like a Jedi, he was planning his escape. The only problem was the sheer impossibility of it. He had never seen so many guards for one prison. There were few exits that he could see. The prison itself was a square inside a square. The cells were in the interior, and the food hall was in the outer square in one corner. They left every day and marched down an underground tunnel to the factory. There didn't seem to be any laundry facilities and the prisoners who had been here for some time looked half-dead and wore rags.

He had seen upon arrival — because they'd wanted him to see it — that the prison was set on a small planet with a dense jungle surrounding it. There were no cities or spaceports, only the small landing platform outside the prison and a larger spaceport floating within the inner atmosphere above.

It was clear that his only opportunity to escape would hinge on the factory. They were forced to work and production levels were high. Obviously what they were doing was more than busy work; it was important to the Empire. That meant there would be a regular pickup service and a delivery supply service, most likely the same ship. That ship would be his way out. Somehow.

He would have to wait to discover the routine. He'd keep his head down, follow the rules, and not make a stir.

He wished he'd kept his lightsaber. He had handed it to Solace, knowing they would have taken it when they captured him. He couldn't bear the thought that his lightsaber, the lightsaber that had once been Garen Muln's, would be tossed on a pile with the hundreds of others, lying on a floor in a storage room at the Temple. He had seen that pile, each lightsaber representing a life, and it had been a heartbreaking sight.

Ferus adopted the shuffle-walk of the other prisoners. He didn't try to catch anyone's eye. He didn't speak. He could tell that the silence would get on his nerves after a while. He had never considered himself a social creature, but he'd come to realize after he left the Jedi that a life of solitude was not for him. He didn't like to live inside his own head.

The prisoners were kept on starvation rations. When they'd arrived, they were each run through a bio-scanner that determined the minimum nutrition their bodies needed to survive. Then their meals were calibrated by droids and individually dished out. That left them with just enough strength to work.

By the time the midday meal came, they were ravenous. Still they had to walk slowly and stay in line as they slid their trays along a long counter. Droids served the food, first flashing a scanner at the ID tag on their uniforms. This gave them the nutrition count for the inmate. They then used a machine to dish out some sort of mealy glop and another equally mysterious portion of something.

Still, it was nourishment, and Ferus found his

mouth watering. He would eat whatever was given to him, because he'd need his strength when the time came.

The droid wheeled around, stuck a spoon in a large tin, then wheeled back and deposited it on Ferus's tray. Then another scoop of the other mass, whatever it was. Ferus didn't care. He began to shuffle forward, keeping his eyes on the back of the neck of the prisoner in front of him. They would all file to long benches at tables and would have a few minutes to eat.

He was so intent on the idea of food — he could not remember the last time he ate a meal — it must have been at that mangy bar down at the Coruscant crust — that he wasn't alert when suddenly, the prisoner ahead of him turned and, in a movement so smooth it must have been done many times, scooped Ferus's food off his tray onto his own.

But if Ferus was a bit slow, he caught up. He saw in a glance that the inmate was tall, with enormous feet and hands and gray stubble on his skull. In a lightning flash of reflexes, he put one knee in the small of the prisoner's back and one arm around his throat. At the same time, he grabbed the food with the other hand and scooped it back onto his tray.

Lunch might be disgusting, but he wasn't about to miss it.

The prisoner in front of him gagged from the

pressure on his throat and tripped. His own tray went flying. Quickly Ferus released his hold and by the time the guard turned he was staring down at the floor, mimicking the exhausted shuffle of the others.

"Keep moving!" The guard lifted his force pike and brought it down on the prisoner's shoulder. He fell, dropping his tray as he went down. Still he reached for the food, even as one arm dangled uselessly. Maliciously the guard kicked the tray away so that he couldn't reach it.

Ferus kept on walking. He ate his food quickly. He had been lucky, he decided. The scene had been over quickly and the guards hadn't seen him.

The prisoners lined up again to walk to the factory. Ferus felt someone behind him and realized it was his cellmate.

"That was a mistake." The tone was low and guttural behind him.

Ferus spoke softly out of the side of his mouth. "At least I kept my lunch."

"Your lunch is the least of your problems, my friend. You just tangled with Prisoner 67. Your problems are just beginning."

CHAPTER FIVE

Trever felt the impact of the water against his ribs and his teeth. He lost his breath and his ability to think. It was like hitting a wall. Everything was black, and he lost consciousness for a moment.

Somehow, Oryon kept hold of him. When he came to he was still against the Bothan's body. They were plummeting down into the dark water. He could feel Oryon's long tangled hair swirling around him like water snakes and was conscious of only one thought:

Up.

He didn't want to die underwater.

Oryon began to fight the momentum pushing them downward. Trever could feel the effort in every muscle. He himself felt as though he had lost control of his own body. He had never felt so helpless.

He felt Oryon's struggle to move toward air. He was kicking his powerful legs but his arms were still wrapped around Trever. With an enormous effort of will, Trever pushed himself away and began to kick on his own. Oryon kept hold of one of his arms, but now with one arm free he was able to make more progress. In this lopsided fashion they managed to stroke their way up.

They surfaced in a burning landscape. Trever gulped down air that tasted of smoke and burning fabric. He didn't know how to swim, but he was able to keep himself afloat, treading water frantically. Dead stormtroopers and pieces of shattered white armor littered the water, though most had sunk below.

"Not so much motion," Oryon said, trying to catch his breath. "You'll tire yourself out."

Trever discovered that he was able to stay up without using as much energy. He didn't like water — never had — but here he was. *Acceptance is the key to survival. Actually, it could be the key to everything.*

Hey, thanks, Feri-Wan, Trever thought. *Maybe there's something to that Jedi stuff after all.*

"We have to find Solace," Oryon said.

It had been a tremendous fall, but they both had no doubt she was alive.

He found he was able to paddle behind Oryon. They passed chunks of floating wreckage, but it was too hot to touch and offered no perch to rest. They searched through the blackness for Solace. All

Trever could see was burning material and black water. Twisted metal still hung overhead, threatening to crash down on them at any moment.

"Over here," Oryon grunted. After a moment of paddling, Trever saw what he'd spotted — someone clinging to a piece of wreckage.

The man was so blackened and bloody it took Trever a moment to realize it was Keets.

"I thought you were dead," Trever said as they made their way up to him.

Keets opened his eyes. "You mean I'm not?"

"Not yet," Oryon said.

Keets was clearly exhausted and in pain. "I slid down the leg of the scaffold and fell in. Surprised I didn't drown. This almost fell on top of me. It's probably the only thing out here that floats. So . . . what's the plan?"

"Find Solace," Oryon said. "She's got to have an escape route."

"That doesn't sound like much of a plan," Keets observed, wincing.

"Okay," Oryon said dryly, "now I know you'll live. You're giving me a hard time already."

A ripple in the dark water made them tense and draw closer to the wreckage. Trever knew they were all thinking of the giant sea creatures they'd glimpsed on the long climb on the catwalks when they'd arrived. No doubt the creatures had dived deeper to escape the fire on the water, but there was always a chance that an inquisitive — or hungry — creature would return for lunch.

Then a dark head surfaced and they breathed a sigh of relief.

"Ready to get out of here?" Solace asked.

"I'd say so," Keets said.

"The others?" Solace asked.

Oryon shook his head. Keets's face tightened.

"They attacked so quickly," he said. "Hume died trying to save a group they surrounded. Rhya . . ."

"I saw her die," Trever whispered.

"Gilly and Spence went to the rear flank. That's where the heaviest fighting was," Oryon said. "They couldn't have survived. And Curran was caught in a firestorm when they torched the houses."

Keets shook his head. "Poor Curran. He was just a kid."

"We'll get out," Solace said. "We can get to my transport. It's not far —" She broke off suddenly. "Wait."

It took them a few seconds longer, but they heard it — the whirring sound of an air speeder. They took refuge behind the wreckage, ducking in back of it as the silver craft zoomed over their heads and made a precarious landing on a partially collapsed catwalk directly over their heads.

"Malorum," Solace breathed.

The commander of the stormtroopers hurried forward, trying to look purposeful despite the fact that he was picking his way carefully. It was clear he didn't quite trust the buckled catwalk.

They could hear the voices overhead echoing off the cavern walls. "Report," Malorum snapped.

"Over half our force has been lost —"

"I don't care about your losses. Where are the rebels?"

"We wiped out the community, sir. Including the Erased we were tracking."

"And the one called Solace?"

"Dead, sir."

"Show me the body."

Solace let out a breath.

"She . . . fell, Inquisitor Malorum. Into the sea."

"Did you see her fall?"

"Yes sir."

"Did you see her drown?"

"I saw her go into the water. . . ."

"Get some lights down there!" Malorum roared. "I want a body!"

Within moments, powerful halo lights began to sweep the dark water.

"We've got to swim for it, and fast," Solace whispered. "Underwater. Oryon, you take Trever and I'll take Keets." She handed out Aquata breathers to Keets and Trever. Oryon had one of his own.

"Nobody has to take me," Keets protested, but it was clear that he needed help.

"Don't argue — it gets on my nerves," Solace said, hooking an arm around his chest. "Ready?"

Oryon hooked an arm around Trever. "Ready."

Taking a deep breath, they slipped beneath the surface as the lights crisscrossed the water. More and more lights appeared, penetrating the water, and Trever couldn't see how they would escape. Solace swam deeper, her powerful legs kicking. Suddenly blaster fire ripped into the water ahead of them. Something exploded behind them. The stormtroopers were shooting into the water randomly, probably on Malorum's orders. And they were sending down explosive devices as well.

It was impossible, Trever thought, twisting through the cold water with Oryon. The water was so cold he could barely feel his feet or hands. He knew his body was failing him. Solace continued to stroke ahead, but he could feel Oryon tiring. Even a Bothan couldn't keep up with a Jedi. And there were too many lights now to get to Solace's ship without being seen.

He didn't know how he found the strength to go on, but watching Solace's strength somehow helped him. When she felt them flagging, she swam behind them and hooked a line onto Oryon's belt, then swam forward, Keets now on her back, his eyes closed. With immense effort, she pulled all of them through the water.

When they finally surfaced, they were far from the scaffolding where the stormtroopers were searching. They could see the lights play on the water far down the tunnel.

Solace stared back at the demolished community.

"I'm sorry," Oryon said.

"It's all right," Solace said. "Nothing lasts. I prepared for this day. If I hadn't been away, I could have gotten them all out. I had a plan . . . but they had a spy. It was Duro. My trusted assistant. It had to be. They got to him — offered him money, threatened him — and he agreed to betray us. He was the only one except me who knew about the warning system. He must have turned it off."

"I'm afraid you're right," Oryon said. "I saw Duro being given a speeder to escape in."

Solace's mouth tightened as she stared down at the smoke and fire. She turned back to them, her face now expressionless. "So you see, it was my mistake that killed them. I trusted him."

"There is always a reason to have only two to share information," Oryon pointed out. "Any more and you greatly increase the risk of betrayal. It's a first rule of a resistance. Information isn't shared."

"I know. I chose the wrong person to trust."

"Traitors exist everywhere."

Solace made an impatient move, reluctant to keep the discussion going.

"Keets, are you conscious?"

"Of course I'm conscious," he growled. "Would I miss all the fun?"

"Can you make it a little farther? You all will have to swim on your own for about twenty meters. I have a duplicate ship hidden underwater, but I have to get there alone. My last resort. I guess we've reached it."

Keets was able to smile wanly. "If ever there was a last resort, this is it."

"I'll help Keets, too," Oryon said.

Trever made a silent vow that if they made it to safety, somehow he would learn how to swim. He felt like a baby bird, flapping his arms and legs, desperately trying to propel himself. He was making progress, but at every moment he was certain if he hadn't been tethered to Oryon, he would sink.

Oryon moved more slowly, more cumbersomely through the water now, saddled with Keets and Trever. Solace had disappeared. Trever saw how Keets was straining to make himself light in the water, keep himself moving. The effort, Trever saw, was exhausting him. Keets' skin was so pale it shone like a pallid moon. His mouth was stretched over his teeth in a grimace. He was shaking uncontrollably.

Still, he kept kicking his legs, swimming to safety, pushing his body past his own endurance.

Just when Trever thought he would gladly give up and sink under the cold water, they saw the glint of durasteel and suddenly the starship was above them, hovering. They could see Solace in the pilot's seat. The ramp lowered, just above the surface of the water, and Oryon pushed Keets onto it. He managed to crawl forward until Solace slipped down and picked him up easily, gently, and brought him aboard.

Trever felt Oryon's push and scrambled up onto the ramp awkwardly, as if he had hooves instead of feet. He tumbled into the cockpit. Oryon followed. He had abandoned his boots in the water and was barefoot, his furred feet bloodied. They fell more than sat in the cockpit seats. Solace had placed Keets on a bunk.

Without a word, she pushed the engines and they shot out through the cavern. Trever didn't know where they were headed . . . and he was too exhausted to care.

CHAPTER SIX

Escape would feel good right about now. If only Ferus could figure out how to accomplish it. Without a lightsaber, he would have to be much more resourceful. And that, of course, was the problem. He was running out of resources, fast. Including his own strength.

Ferus had been here for only two days, but already he was feeling the effects of too little sleep, not enough food, and crushing, repetitive work.

Every day they were marched into a factory. Ferus could see that it had been recently built, perhaps shortly after Palpatine had declared himself Emperor. It had been thrown up hastily, so there were already cracks in the floor and ceiling, cracks that let in both a stinging rain and a barrage of fat, hungry insects with strong pincers that drew blood.

If you flinched, you received a blow from the guards, so you learned never to flinch. You worked.

Ferus couldn't tell what they were manufacturing, only that it was a piece of something larger. The inmates were switched day to day from one task to another. Were they working on weapons? Machinery? Droids? The parts were too small or too obscure to tell. There were murmurs about an "ultimate weapon," but Ferus couldn't figure out what it could be.

Every so often prisoners were pulled off the line and taken away, and no one ever saw them again. Ferus knew his days were numbered. He would die at the whim of Malorum. Most likely the Inquisitor was delaying his execution just to make him suffer.

Everyone avoided him now. His cellmate planned to fake an illness to get into the infirmary. Ferus spoke to him just before lights out.

"But you said that nobody who gets transferred there ever gets out," Ferus reminded his cellmate in a whisper.

"I'd rather be killed with a shot in the arm by a med droid than be caught in the crossfire with you," he answered.

"Listen," Ferus said, "I can handle myself. And I don't intend to die here."

His cellmate looked at him, his tired gaze rueful. "You're one of those who think they can escape. All the more reason for me to go. You're trouble because you don't get it. There's no way out."

"There's always a way out."

"Well." The cellmate stretched out his legs and laughed. "You have your way and I have mine."

His laugh, to Ferus, was the loneliest sound in the galaxy, a winter wind on a world of high deserts. He could hear in that laugh the sound of someone ready to die.

Four guards came and escorted him out roughly. Ferus watched him go with sorrow. He had a feeling that in another life, he would have liked his cellmate's company. He had never known his name.

Morning. Or, at least, he guessed it was morning. He hadn't seen the sun since he'd arrived. Or the moon or the sky. All this duracrete was starting to get to him. He was locked in a world of gray rock. He could see around him how the skin tones of the others, even the blue or green skin of other species, were all turning gray.

He waited for the sound of the automatic lock that snapped simultaneously on all the cells. They were then expected to file out within three seconds or find the end of a force pike jabbed in their ribs.

He pulled on his boots and stood by the door,

waiting. Today, he decided. Today something had to change. He had to find something — a weak link in the chain, a sloppy guard, an unguarded door. Today would be the first day taken toward escape.

The locks snapped; the start of another back-breaking day.

Ferus stepped out into the corridor and they were on him immediately. He had felt no surge of danger.

Prisoner 67 and five of his henchmen surrounded him in a bloc and pushed him forward into the lineup. Prisoner 67 slipped immediately behind him. Out of the corner of his eye, Ferus saw that 67's enormous hands were poised to wrap around his throat. Meanwhile, unseen by the guards, the other four pressed close to Ferus, keeping his arms pinned to his sides. He could feel the surprising strength of their grip. Obviously stealing food from other inmates had its advantages.

Ferus understood his problem immediately, in a flash that gave him every option, recalling his Jedi training. He had no weapon. He had no means of escape, for if he stepped out of line the guards would kill him as easily as a slug — he'd seen it happen.

If he fought Prisoner 67 — which, of course, he meant to do — he was certain that 67's henchmen would simply step aside, break up the shield, and watch as Ferus was taken away by the guards.

Attacking another prisoner could yield several different results, all of them bad. You could be hauled away to be tortured or just killed on the spot. It just depended on the mood of the guards. And they were always in bad moods.

All of this ran through Ferus's mind in less time than it took for Prisoner 67 to step squarely behind him. 67's hands came up — big, meaty slabs capable of crushing Ferus's windpipe.

Ferus decided to use a Jedi combat method, what one of his instructors had called "attacking backward." He would reverse an offensive move and fight his attacker without ever turning to engage him. Fun in a classroom fighting against other Padawans, but somehow in a brutal prison where anything goes . . . not so fun.

Ferus gave a sudden twist and a hard jab, loosening the grip of the prisoners next to him. But 67 was just as quick. One thick forearm wrapped around his throat. Ferus felt his vision go gray.

Suddenly out of the corner of his eye he saw something — a flicker, a glimmer — that translated quickly into the sight of a plastoid datacard winging through the air with incredible velocity and spin. Its speed was so fast it was almost invisible. Ferus ducked and it hit Prisoner 67 in the center of the forehead. His eyes rolled up and he fell heavily.

The guards heard the thump and rushed toward

the sound, but by the time they reached it Ferus had already melted forward a few steps. Even the henchmen, though stunned, were able to merge with the crowd.

The indifferent guards dragged the body away.

Ferus searched the crowd without seeming to look, a Jedi technique. Whoever his rescuer was, he couldn't see him. He had rejoined the crowd. Ferus could see the other prisoners' eyes moving, also searching. No one had seen the source of the silent attack.

Baffled, Ferus marched into the factory with the others. Another day of grueling work.

Another meal of slop.

But he had something now he didn't have before. There were only a few in the galaxy who had the skill and the knowledge to turn a datacard into a lethal weapon, who could throw it from that distance without being seen.

One of them was his friend.

It was near the end of the day, as he was standing by a noisy machine, feeding bits of durasteel into it to create continuous sheets and trying not to get his fingers cut off in the process, when he heard a familiar voice directly behind him.

"Fancy meeting you here, Olin. Thought you preferred classier joints."

Ferus grinned without turning. "Your kind of place, Flax," he murmured under his breath.

His rescuer had been exactly who he'd hoped he was. Clive Flax — lowlife musician. Industrial spy. Double agent.

Things were looking up.

CHAPTER SEVEN

The passageways were so narrow they had to abandon the speeder, hiding it behind some trash-compacting machines. They didn't think they could take another step, but Oryon, Solace, Keets, and Trever kept walking. Trever couldn't remember the last time he'd slept or eaten. Time was a blur, and fatigue was lead in his bones.

Solace had meandered around the levels of Coruscant, hoping to stir up any possible surveillance so that she could identify it. Only when she was sure they weren't being trailed did she follow Oryon's directions to Dexter Jettster's secret hideout.

It was in the very outskirts of the Orange District. The district had received its nickname when its inhabitants had continually changed the glowlights to orange, despite the efforts of Coruscant Utilities to keep the clear white glow intended to discourage crime. Those in the Orange District didn't care much about crime. They preferred the dim glow of privacy.

It had been only a few days since Trever had first been here with Ferus, searching for Dexter Jettster and hoping he could give them information on a missing Jedi. It seemed like a lifetime ago now.

Oryon led them down a narrow alleyway under the eerie orange light. The buildings here were smoothly rounded at the corners and no higher than ten or twelve stories, unusual on Coruscant. They gave the impression of gentle hills if you squinted hard, but if you really looked you realized that the lack of windows made them creepy. Trever could see the slits in the walls that served as lookouts. He felt the strong sensation of being watched.

Every time he thought they had come to the end of the alley, it turned another way or doubled back on itself. The buildings seemed to hang over them closer and closer as they walked.

On Coruscant you grew used to the constant noise, the hum of speeders and conversations and the whirr of airbuses. The quiet here was unnerving. They could hear their footsteps and their breathing.

Oryon stopped in front of a dwelling identical to all the others they had passed. He hesitated outside the door. Trever was about to ask why when he realized that Oryon was allowing whoever was inside to see him clearly, as well as his companions. Then he walked forward and punched in a code at the door. It slid open almost immediately.

They entered a hallway lit dimly by powered-down glowlights. A ramp led to an upper level; Oryon climbed it, motioning them to follow. He walked down another hallway, this one wider, but with an odd combination of clinical and military objects. A durasteel cart rested against one wall and a pile of weapons was neatly arranged in a rack. A shelf of medicines rested on a tray. Trever didn't know if he was in a hospital or a barracks.

Oryon accessed a door midway down the hall. Dexter Jettster sat on a chair that was reinforced to accommodate his bulk. Against one wall was a sole bare table. The far, opposite wall was entirely filled up with security screens. In a glance Trever could see that they effectively covered the entire alley-way, the roof, the houses next door, the sky above, and the entrance to the alley, at least two kilometers away.

Dexter raised himself from the chair and lowered his head, tilting it toward them in a way that Trever remembered from his last meeting. It signaled Dex's surrender to deep emotion.

"Glad to see you." He nodded at Solace. "Happy to see you survived." He scanned them. "But not all of you made it back."

Oryon spoke first. "We know Rhya and Hume are

dead. Gilly and Spence — we believe so. And Curran as well."

Dex shook his head. "No, no, not the wily Curran. He's not dead."

"I'm sorry," Oryon said. "It's impossible that he could have survived —"

"Impossible? No. Improbable, yes. He's here — a little the worse for wear, mind you. He stole an Imperial speeder and met a wall with some force, but he'll do just fine. Looked a bit like Keets there when he arrived. Come on then. I have a med center, if you can call it that. A med droid to take care Keets, and food for everyone."

Dex led them to a blank wall and waved his hand over a portion of it. The wall slid back.

Curran sat up in a med pod while a droid checked his vitals. His furred face lit up when he saw them.

"Keets! I saw you hit."

"They can hit me, but they can't kill me," Keets replied.

The med droid rolled closer, its sensors blinking. "Weak vitals. Sit on pod."

Keets moved to a pod next to Curran and sat. "Gladly."

"We'll leave you to it," Dex said. "If you're cleared to join us, we'll be in the galley."

"I'll be cleared," Keets promised.

"Negative, vitals too weak," the droid said.

"I'll be cleared, you clanking heartless hunk of sensors," Keets said. "Now fix me up, quick." He lay back and closed his eyes, finally giving in to the exhaustion and the pain.

After they got to the hallway, Dex chuckled. "He looks half-dead, that Keets, but I wager he'll be up and about in no time. Now come this way. I've been cooking up my special relish, and I can still dish up some sliders."

Trever pushed away his third helping. Dex had insisted that they not discuss what was happening while they ate, and although it had been hard for all of them, they'd managed to eat something without their stomachs churning. Trever was still worried about Ferus, furious and scared, but at least he'd managed to eat. Dex had regaled them with stories during their meal, stories about the street they were living on. It was called Thugger's Alley, using sub-level Coruscant slang for lowlifes and thieves. Nobody on the outside was quite sure who lived there; mostly they kept their distance.

Dex, however, knew who lived here. Some low-lifes, surely, he said with a chuckle, but more of those like the Erased, those who despised what the Emperor represented and declined to live under his rules. So they set up elaborate security and so far the Empire had left them alone.

"Of course we can't fight them," Dex said. "But we'll see them coming."

"I wish I could say the same," Solace said.

"Now, enough of that," Dex said kindly. "No looking back, isn't that the Jedi way?"

"Something like that," she replied. Her gaze was remote.

"Hmm . . . what's next to do, then? You don't know where they took Ferus?"

"Just that he was arrested." Trever felt his stomach lurch. He shouldn't have eaten all those sliders after all. They felt sour in his stomach now.

One of Dex's four hands came down on his shoulder with surprising gentleness. "There isn't a place in the galaxy we can't find him, so don't you worry."

"That's right," Solace said. "We'll start with likely prisons and move out from there. We'll need transports; I don't have a hyperdrive on my ship."

"Transports we can get for you," Dex said.

"That's a random plan," Trever pointed out. "By the time you find him, he could be executed a dozen times. What we need is information."

Solace looked at him, startled. She wasn't used to being questioned, he guessed. But if a plan was stupid, somebody had to say so, in his opinion.

"Do you have a better idea?" she asked, looking down her nose at him.

Trever felt his irritation flare. "Just give me a minute — it won't be hard."

"Now hold on here," Dex said. "Solace, with due respect, Trever is right. If you go from prison to prison, it could take years. The Empire has more prisons than banthas have ticks. What we need is infiltration."

Trever noticed that Curran and Keets had quietly entered the room. Curran looked stronger, his glossy hair now smoothed and pulled back into the thick metal ring. His small, furred face was alert. Keets had a bacta bandage on his side and winced as he sat down in a chair.

"It's time for exposure," Dex said.

He looked at Oryon, Keets, and Curran. "We've lost good friends on this day," he continued. "The other Erased have gone underground again. I have a sweet spot here, and you're welcome to share it. It'd be safe, I guarantee that, at least until the Empire feels like looking for us. Then we'll find another. But . . ." Dex paused. "It's time to join the fight, my friends. To fight means you have to risk exposure. We need to resurface."

Curran nodded. "I was thinking the same thing."

"I've still got my contacts in the Senate," Keets said.

"And there are a few even in the Imperial Army officer corps who don't like where they are," Oryon added. "They might talk."

"I've got friends I can ask, too," Dex said. "If we do this, we could attract the notice of the Inquisitors. They'll come looking, no doubt about that."

The others nodded. They would accept that risk.

"But why?" Trever asked them. "You hardly know Ferus. You just met him a few days ago."

"Doesn't matter," Dex said. "We're all soldiers in the same fight now. We'll risk what we have to for our own."

Trever looked at Dex gratefully. He knew Ferus would be touched by their help. He only hoped Ferus would live long enough to see it.

CHAPTER EIGHT

That night, Ferus's cell door slid open and the guards threw a body inside. Ferus sat up, leaning on his elbows. The door slid shut and Clive unfolded himself from his tucked position. He dusted off his dirty prison coveralls.

"I don't know why they have to do that," he said.

"How'd you manage it?" Ferus whispered.

"There's a creepy logic to this regime," Clive answered in a low tone, settling himself next to Ferus. It had been at least two years since Ferus had last seen him. He was thinner, and his thick black hair was cut close to his head. His blue eyes had dark smudges underneath them. Then again, they all looked older.

"When you rule by fear, everyone is afraid of you," Clive said, lying back and crossing one ankle over his knee. "This can have its advantages.

Obviously. I mean, they're in control of the galaxy, right? But it can offer windows of opportunity for fellows like me. Hence. There's a chap in the data-works section — not an Imperial guy, just a civilian with a job. He had a slight problem with his program, and I saw him sweat. If you mess up on the job here, you get a boot in the face and a transfer to someplace worse. Does that concept boggle the mind or what? So I fixed it for him on the sly. He owed me a favor. This is it."

"So what are you in for?" Ferus asked.

Clive stretched out his legs. "I was lying low under one of your excellent false identities — thanks for never charging me, by the way — when I saw an opportunity I couldn't pass up."

"Don't tell me. A little espionage? A tiny theft of an industrial secret?"

Clive grinned. "Something along those lines. The next thing I knew, I was being arrested. They threw me against a wall and put stun cuffs on me. They traced my ID docs and somehow in a burst of their usual efficiency they discovered who I was. That was act three of this space opera, mate. Once they had my real name, they had me. Into the slammer I went. The End."

But it wasn't the end. Ferus knew enough about Clive to know that. He'd met Flax in the time before the Clone Wars, when he was still operating his business, Olin/Lands. He and his partner Roan offered their services to whistleblowers, beings who exposed corruption and then found the law did not protect them. Roan and Ferus created new identities for the whistleblowers and their families and also offered protection while they established themselves on new worlds. Clive hadn't needed their protection — he had honed his own style of defense, with amazing skills Ferus had never seen outside of the Temple.

Using his abilities as a musician, he had often gone unnoticed in bars or parties while he was gathering information or stealing it. It was a living, he would say with a shrug. Once the Clone Wars started, he saw his skills as marketable. Ferus had thought of him immediately after he had been put in charge of an operation on the planet of Jabor. He had recruited Clive and sent him undercover to a Separatist base to work as a double agent. As a result, Ferus had been able to bust a Separatist spy ring that had operated throughout the Mid-Rim. It hadn't won the war, but it had saved lives.

If there was anybody in the galaxy who he'd want to watch his back — with the exception of Roan or Obi-Wan — it was Clive Flax.

"So what's the plan?" Ferus asked.

"What plan?"

"The escape plan. I know you have one."

"You're right," Clive admitted easily. "I just need an accomplice. The galaxy smiled on me the day I saw your ugly mug in here. That's why I kept you alive."

"You mean you only saved my life so you could use me?"

"Of course, mate. You know I only think about my own sweet self." Clive grinned at him.

"Tell me the plan," Ferus said. "I don't care what it is — I'm in."

"I've been stealing things for months," Clive said. He reached inside his coveralls and laid out several items on the hard floor.

Ferus looked at them dubiously.

A servodriver.

A spoon.

A droid's restraining bolt.

A handful of durasteel bits.

"This is what you're going to break out of prison with?"

Clive picked up one of the tiny bits. "You see this? You put a small object in a piece of equipment in the right way, you can disable it. Disable something, you've got a distraction. Sometimes that's all you need." He replaced the scrap of metal with something like fondness. "Besides, I had a plastoid datacard, too, but I had to use it to save your sorry neck. The transport ship comes tomorrow for the new load. Are you in or out?"

Ferus gave another glance at the motley group of objects. Sure, they didn't look like much. But Clive had just saved his life with a datacard.

"I'm in," he said.

CHAPTER NINE

Malorum sat in the cockpit of his private starship on one of the landing platforms of Polis Massa.

There were too many unrelated facts in his brain. He was used to cataloging facts and swiftly reaching conclusions — that's how smart he was — but now he felt only confusion. He hated confusion.

Think, he told himself impatiently.

He suspected that Senator Amidala had been treated here, but he could not locate any evidence of it.

One of his best agents, Sancor, had been killed here. According to the operational head of the med-center, Maneeli Tuun, Sancor had "accidentally" fallen off an observation platform and landed on some lethally sharp surgical instruments.

Accident. Did they take him for a fool?

A source had told him that a Jedi had been the one to take Amidala's body to Naboo. Of course the galaxy believed the Jedi had killed Amidala, but Malorum knew it was a lie fabricated to slur the Jedi. He didn't care about that. He cared only about what really happened, because it was information Darth Vader did not have. And any information Vader didn't have could be used against him.

The funeral . . .

Malorum tapped his fingers against the cockpit instrument panel. The funeral had been organized in haste. For such a ceremonial people, it was perhaps too hasty.

He leaned over to the nav computer. He set a course for Naboo. His work here was finished. He'd found nothing.

Instinct was telling him that his answers lay there, not with Ferus Olin. He would call in the execution order. The galaxy would have one less Jedi sympathizer in it.

That could only be an improvement.

CHAPTER TEN

Trever walked down a warehouse aisle, in between blocks of towering garbage. The smell was overpowering. He could see fat white gaberworms as long as his arm slithering through the waste.

Workers of many species toiled without stopping, shoveling the garbage into a machine that cubed and sanitized it. They wore face masks and gloves, but Trever couldn't imagine that those helped with the smell or the feel of the garbage.

"Told you you'd regret tagging along," Keets told him.

"It's not so bad," Trever said. "You should have seen my brother's bedroom."

The joke slipped out before he could stop it. Keets gave him a quick, sharp look. He hadn't mentioned his family before. He never mentioned his family. Their lives, their deaths, were his business.

He hated to think about them. He tried not to. It

was tough coming from a family of heroes and martyrs. His mother, his father, and his brother had all fought the Empire. They had all been killed. He had no intention of ending as they did, if he could help it.

He sensed the itch in Keets to ask another question — he was a journalist, after all — but Keets said nothing, just kept leading the way down the aisle of the facility toward the friend he called Davis Joness.

Keets had filled Trever in on the background as they took an airbus fifty levels down to the facility. Davis Joness had been an influential and powerful Coruscant administrator. He had remained neutral during the Clone Wars but could not conceal his distaste for the Empire's new regulations. One day, he ran afoul of the new Imperial leadership and was instantly reassigned to garbage duty.

They found him at the end of the line, using a servoshovel to pick up the hunks of garbage that had fallen from the piles. He wore a bright orange bandanna around his head and boots up to his thighs. His eyebrows shot up over his face mask when he caught sight of Keets.

"Come to give me a hand?" he asked.

"I think I'll pass."

"You disappeared."

"Thought it might be a good idea at the time."

"Why'd you come back?"

"Usual story. I missed all this." Keets lifted his arms to take in the towers of garbage.

"Come on — we can't talk here, there are spies everywhere." Davis stripped off his gloves and tossed them onto a pile of reeking garbage.

They followed him through a green door to an outside courtyard. Trever took a deep breath of fresher air, trying not to be obvious about it. Unfortunately, Davis smelled almost as bad as the garbage he handled. There was no fresh air to be had in his vicinity.

Davis noticed when Trever moved away slightly. "Occupational hazard," he said. With a sigh, he sat down on an upended cone of permacrete that served as a stool. "Glad to see a face from the old days, anyway," he said.

"You gave me some great tips in the past," Keets said. "Are you still hooked in?"

"Sure, I still keep my fingers on the pulse of Senatorial high jinks," Davis said with a half-smile. "I just can't help myself. It's a blast watching the Senators debate about how many meters wide the Coruscant flag should be while the Emperor plans more death and destruction."

"So tell me: Where do they send the political prisoners? The worst of the worst?"

"Don't you mean the best of the best?"

Keets inclined his head, conceding the point.

"I've heard about a new prison world. Dontamo. A work prison. The most elite prisoners are sent there. If you know someone who ends up within its walls, forget them. Everybody works and everybody dies."

Trever clasped his hands behind his back and squeezed, trying to distract himself from believing it.

"It's not safe here," Davis told Keets, suddenly looking around. "You'd better go. There are at least three workers here who pass along information. Those are the ones I know about. Your image was taken as you entered; they'll put it through security if one of the workers tips them off, which they will."

"I'm already on Malorum's bad side," Keets said. "I doubt it can get worse."

"Well, you're in luck. He's on Naboo for the moment, or so I hear. But you'd better get lost anyway."

Keets turned to go. Then he turned back again. "Why do you stay?"

"I've been barred from every profession except this one. I've got kids." He balled his fingers into fists and stared at them, his eyes bloodshot, his face mottled red from exposure to garbage toxins. "What else can I do?"

When Trever and Keets returned, Oryon and Curran were talking to Dex. Solace was studying a holographic star chart.

"We worked a contact in the air control," Oryon said. "A starship left the landing platform of a Coruscant high-security prison yesterday. It was headed for the Radiant One system."

"We've been reading the star charts," Dex said. "We can narrow it down to about fifteen prisons. Radiant One is a big system, well beyond the Core."

"We're trying out probability theories, trying to rank them in importance so we know where to start," Curran added.

Trever looked at Keets. They'd already looked up Dontamo on the star charts. It was in Radiant One. This was the confirmation they needed.

"You don't need to look any longer," Keets told the others. "We know where he is." He strode over to the star chart and pointed his finger. "Here."

"There's something else you should know," Dex said reluctantly. "An execution order has gone through for Ferus."

Silence suddenly filled the room. Trever closed his eyes as he felt them burn. *Not again. Not again. Not again.*

Not someone he cared about dying at the hands of the Empire.

"No," he said fiercely, surprised he'd spoken aloud. "We'll get there in time."

"I can make it in half a day," Solace said.

"We're coming with you," Oryon and Curran said at the same time.

Solace looked at them, surprised.

"We're seeing this through," Keets said.

"It's like Dex told us," Oryon said. "It's time to join the fight."

CHAPTER ELEVEN

The plan was simple. The hard part was doing it.

Ferus lay awake in the darkness, reviewing what Clive had outlined while Clive himself slept in a corner snoring loudly.

Once they were at the factory, Clive would disable a loading machine that transported the huge durasteel cartons onto the transport ship. He simply planned to disable the counting system. The fact that he swore he would be able to do this with a spoon was enough to give Ferus nightmares, so he chose not to dwell on that.

"Inventory," Clive had said, explaining his plan. "If you mess up their inventory procedures, they go crazy. They know they're accountable to some Grand Moffing Toffhead down the line, so it has to be spot-on. So the crates are being loaded, but they're not being counted. That means they're going to have to do a manual count. Which means they'll flip open the bay doors on the transport. And that will give us our chance. After you take care of the main guard and grab his weapon —"

"How am I going to do that?"

"You'll think of something. The other guards will be checking out the machine and watching the prisoners, because when something goes wrong, they're afraid everyone will riot."

"So I take out the guard . . ."

"By that time I'll be in position to stop the loader completely. Then you and I get on board using the bay doors, get to the cockpit, throw out the pilots, and take off."

"There seem to be a number of holes in this plan."

"Well, nothing's perfect."

Ferus thought back on the conversation now as he lay on his back. He trusted Clive, he trusted his instincts — and he also trusted that if he didn't take this opportunity, he'd be dead.

He closed his eyes but didn't sleep. It was before dawn when he heard the boots outside. Too early to roust the prisoners for the day.

He could see the gleam in Clive's eyes. He was wide-awake, listening. "This can't be good," Clive whispered.

The boots stopped outside the door. Clive moved

fast. He threw himself across the cell and punched Ferus just as the door flew open and the lights were powered up suddenly in an attempt to blind them.

"He stole my boots!" Clive shouted wildly.

"Doesn't matter now," the guard smirked.

Ferus was picked up and thrown into a transport cart, a small, locking box they used to move prisoners in and out . . . to the execution bloc.

It was his time.

The cover closed and locked. Within seconds, they were wheeling Ferus out.

He clutched a restraining bolt in his fingers — the bolt that Clive had passed him when he'd pretended to attack him. He had no idea what to do with it. It was hardly a weapon. But it was something.

Ferus was thrown into a cell. His execution order was read out loud to him. "By the order of . . ." "Crimes against the Imperial regime . . ." It didn't matter.

The door locked behind the guards. It was a tiny cell with thick durasteel walls. There was no room to lie down and barely room to sit. There was no window, no chair. Nothing here but time, and very little of that.

He grasped the bolt in his fist. He couldn't break out of here with a bolt. Clive knew that. But when they came for him, when they took him to the execution room, then maybe he could use it.

You put a small object in a piece of equipment in the right way, you can disable it. Disable something, you've got a distraction. Sometimes that's all you need.

All in all, he'd rather have a lightsaber.

Already he heard them coming. They didn't let you sit for long.

He still had the Force. It was here, even on this stinking, dismal planet, even in this dark cage of a room. It was inside him and around him and he could access it whenever he chose.

He stood.

Today he would either die or escape.

It would be his choice. Not theirs.

The door slid open. There were six stormtroopers. One was an officer, consulting a datapad attached to his wrist.

"Ferus Olin, criminal from the planet Bellassa. Retinal scan." He held up a scanner to Ferus's eye. "Identification confirmed."

They pushed him into another room, a larger one, with several chairs with restraints that were bolted to the ceiling and trailed down like lethal vines. There was a med droid in the corner. So it would be lethal injection.

They pushed him past the droid. He palmed the restraining bolt as he passed. He hoped the guards would keep shoving him, and they did, poking him with their blaster rifles. He pretended to stumble and reached out with an arm to steady himself. He grabbed on to the med droid.

"Off!" The stormtrooper slammed the butt of the rifle into his shoulder.

The pain radiated down Ferus's arm. It didn't matter. He'd been able to slip the bolt into the droid's socket.

They brought him toward the chair, then slammed him down into it.

"Prepare injection," the officer said.

The droid didn't move.

"Prepare injection!" the officer snapped.

"Restrained," the droid answered succinctly.

"What?"

The officer turned. It was the moment Ferus had been waiting for. With one kick he sent one stormtrooper into another; an elbow sent a third spinning. The Force hummed around him as he leaped over the pile, snatching up two blasters on the way. He twisted in midair, held himself motionless for one instant to blast the droid to smithereens, then landed. He dived away from blaster fire and used the momentum to roll himself like a ball, taking down the rest of the stormtroopers. On his way up he grabbed a security card out of a stormtrooper's utility belt.

The officer faced him, his blaster held steady.

Ferus held his blasters. Neither of them moved.

The officer fired. Ferus had already taken advantage of the instant before the blast and leaped. He fired above at the ceiling. The bolts holding the restraints in place fell. The restraining cables dropped to the floor. He wrapped the officer in them and fled.

Since he'd been in the restraint box, he wasn't sure where he was in the prison complex. He would have to find the factory. He wasn't sure if Clive had been able to disable the loader but he had to assume that the plan was on schedule. Clive would expect him to show up. If he didn't, he had no doubt that Clive would leave without him . . . if he could.

Ferus ran through the halls. There had to be another entrance to the factory, one for the guards to use.

He found it. The blast doors opened with a swipe of the card. The racket of the factory assaulted his ears.

Glad to kiss this place good-bye.

He ducked behind a machine. The line of prisoners kept their faces toward their work. A guard patrolled — up and down, up and down. Ferus could see no disruption in routine. In the distance, the transport freighter sat, while a conveyor ramp rolled crate after crate inside.

Then he heard the crackle of a transmitter and saw an officer walking quickly down the aisle, toward the freighter. Another officer was hurrying from the opposite direction.

Ferus was covered by the noise of the machines and the regular routine of the patrolling guard. While the guard's back was to him, he rushed forward and took down the first officer. The officer cracked his head on machinery and was out cold.

Keeping his head down, Ferus ran past the clamor of the turbines stamping durasteel into sheets and forming them into gears and pins. He grabbed a handful of gears as he ran.

By now the prisoners had noted him but they said nothing. If one of them was going to break out, he would make it or not make it. They would neither help him nor hinder him. But he could feel their avid interest in his progress and their conviction that he would fail.

The bay doors were open now, and the second officer was striding up the ramp, ready to do the manual count. No doubt he expected his fellow officer at any moment. They had a window of time to do this. Once he was unable to raise the officer on his comlink, the officer would become suspicious.

"About time you showed up." Clive was beside him now.

"Blasters." Ferus said the word not as a need but a warning.

"Wha —"

Ferus had felt the surge in the Force, warning him. He shoved Clive down as the blaster fire exploded overhead. It hit a stamping machine, sending molten fire through it.

"We've been spotted," Ferus said.

"You think?"

They raced up the ramp, zigzagging to avoid the fire from the guards behind them. Stormtroopers appeared and thundered up the ramp. Clive used an old trick, tossing the handful of gears down the ramp. The stormtroopers slipped and fell. With a Force-push, Ferus gave them an extra boost, sending them flying back onto the factory floor.

Clive gave him a surprised look but there was no time for questions. Clive hurled the spoon, end over end over end, toward the sole Imperial officer. It hit him straight in the center of the forehead with such force that the officer's eyes rolled back in his head and he collapsed in a heap. Ferus quickly closed the bay doors.

"Cockpit," Clive said. "They'll be coming after us with the big guns now."

"Those weren't the big guns?"

They raced to the cockpit and barreled through the door. Two freighter pilots stood up from where they'd been lounging with one eye on the nav computer panel. They saw the blaster in Ferus's hand and the determined look in Clive's eyes.

They held up their hands. "I didn't sign on for this," one said.

"Me either," said the other.

"The door's that way," Clive said. He hit the cockpit ramp button with his fist.

They catapulted themselves out, jumping off the ramp before it hit the floor. Clive hit the ramp control again as Ferus fired up the engines.

The freighter ship shot into the sky. The prison became a gray blur in the middle of a jungle.

And then the first starfighters began to rise from the landing platform below.

"Do they have to be so stinking *fast*?" Clive muttered.

"What's the status on our weapons system?" Ferus asked, pushing the speed.

Clive reviewed the computer readouts. "Uh, not great. We've got a couple of low-power laser cannons."

"And?"

"That's it."

"That's it?"

"That's it."

Ferus gave a quick glance at the nav computer. The Imperial starfighters were gaining. The freighter was old and slow. Its weapons were rudimentary. They could play hide-and-seek, but there were no asteroids in the vicinity, and anyway it would be like hiding a Wookiee behind a twig.

"We didn't come this far to be turned into space dust," Clive said fiercely.

But they both looked out at the ships and knew they were doomed.

CHAPTER TWELVE

Trever and the others had kept in touch at first, but as the planet Dontamo drew closer they maintained comm silence. Even if they scrambled communications, they didn't want Imperial scouts to pick up anything.

Dex had pulled in a major favor and outfitted them with two small starships. They had seen service in the Clone Wars and their hulls were battered and pockmarked with the ghosts of small asteroid collisions and missile fire. But the engines were tweaked and their hyperdrives had been overhauled.

Trever, Keets, and Solace were in one modified ARC-170 starfighter, Oryon and Curran in an overhauled Jedi starfighter. Their plan was not much of a plan, in Trever's opinion, but they didn't have a choice. They simply had to land and see what they found. There was no time to obtain the prison specs, no time for surveillance. If an execution order had been issued, the small group of combatants had to move as fast as they could and take their chances.

Trever kept his eyes on the nav computer. He was alert for any signs of Imperial patrol ships. Oryon had told him that they often did routine inspections of the airspace surrounding the prison worlds. Every nerve inside him was screaming to land and find Ferus.

Suddenly he sat forward. "Something's going on. Look." He pointed to the dots on the computer. "A ship is being chased."

"A freighter, by the looks of it." Solace keyed in a few strokes. "And those are starfighters."

"Imperial starfighters chasing an old freighter? Why?"

"Not our problem. Could be good news for us," Solace said. "They'll be distracted by whatever's going on, and we can —"

She stopped abruptly.

"What is it?" Solace's face had suddenly gone still and tight, a look Trever was becoming familiar with.

"The Force. Something . . ." She stared hard at the screen. "Ferus is on that ship." She reached for the comm unit. "Oryon, come in. The ship on XYZ coordinates 1138, 1999, 2300 —"

"We see it."

"Our target is on that ship. And at the controls, by the looks of it."

"Looks like he could use a hand. Let's go."

Trever was suddenly slammed back in his seat as Solace took the fighter into a spinning dive.

"Did I warn you to hang on?" she yelled over the scream of the engines.

Trever felt plastered back against the seat. He had seen Solace's piloting skills, navigating through the tight spaces and close shaves that was Coruscant air traffic. This was combat flying — fast, dangerous. It might have even felt exhilarating, if he hadn't also felt like he was about to die any second.

"You're going to have to operate the laser cannons," Solace told him. "Can you do it?"

"I'm pretty good," Trever said, even though technically he hadn't operated any before.

"Get to it," she said. "Just don't shoot Oryon."

Trever switched on the cannons. He spread his legs, keeping his balance, his eye at the scope. The Imperial fighters were firing on the starfreighter. Compared to the agile fighters, the freighter looked like a gigantic clumsy tractor plowing through stars.

The starfighters hadn't realized the two newcomers were a threat, not yet. They might get a few clear shots first.

Trever lined up a shot. Almost within range. Almost . . . almost. . . .

He pressed the activator —

— and was rewarded with the bloom of smoke from one of the starfighters.

"Good work!" Solace shouted. "Let me get closer. They'll be on us now."

Trever quickly discovered that shooting at a starfighter was much more difficult when the starfighters were engaged in evasive maneuvers . . . and shooting back at him.

Space suddenly erupted in fire. It had bumps and peaks and valleys, currents of percussive bumps that Solace rode with ease, one hand on the controls, the other on her own weaponry controls.

Oryon was looping around the starfighters, peppering them with fire and trying to stay between them and the freighter. Suddenly Ferus's voice popped into their frequency.

"Whoever you are, thank you!" he yelled.

"It's us, sweetcake. Watching your back as usual," Keets's voice boomed out.

"It's good to see you! I owe you one."

"You owe us plenty!" Trever shouted from the gunport.

Oryon's constant blaster hammering hit one starfighter, which spiraled out of control. Now only two were left, and Solace and Oryon proved to be the better pilots, maneuvering their ships so that they boxed the starfighters in, then blasted them.

Fire burst on their wings and fuselage and they careened down toward the prison world.

Ferus's freighter did a lazy circle around them.

"How about a rendezvous point?"

Solace clicked through the possibilities. "How about Alba-16? It's not far, and the Empire has no real presence there."

"And it's got a great cantina!" an unfamiliar voice roared through the comm unit.

"Who was that?" Oryon asked.

Trever felt his heart rise as he heard Ferus's chuckle. It was good to hear it. He couldn't help feeling that everything would be okay.

"Don't ask," Ferus said.

It wasn't until Alba-16 was close that Clive brought up to Ferus what he'd seen. He was sitting in the copilot's chair, boots on the console, leaning back as far as the chair would allow him to go.

"I always thought there was something odd about you, but I never guessed you were a Jedi," he said.

"I was never a Jedi," Ferus corrected. "I left when I was still a Padawan."

"Never heard of one leaving. A story there, eh?" Clive said, but he didn't ask for it. "You could have told me. I would have felt a mite easier about our escape probability factor. As it was, I thought for sure we were going to die."

"My abilities aren't as sharp as they were. And I had no lightsaber. I didn't want you to overestimate what I could do."

"Well, it was a nice surprise, mate. You did all right."

"You didn't have to punch me."

"Authenticity, Master Ferus. That's the key to every escape."

Ferus landed the ship at the Alba-16 spaceport. It held the usual collection of freighters and haulers as well as a few personal craft. Because the planet was without an Imperial garrison, no one questioned the arrival of the ships. Behind him, the two starfighters landed. Solace popped the canopy on hers and a moment later Trever stuck his head out. He jumped out on the wing and leaped to the ground, then ran toward Ferus. Suddenly he stopped, embarrassed. Ferus saw his hands dangling. He knew that Trever wanted to show his feelings, but didn't want to expose them. The boy was such a curious mixture of emotion and toughness.

Ferus had once been a stiff person, too, but not anymore. He slung one arm around Trever's shoulders and gave him a quick, fierce hug. "Thought you lost me, didn't you?"

"You do have a way of cutting things close," Trever said.

The rest of the group walked up.

"Do me a favor," Keets said to Ferus. "Try not to get arrested again."

"Who's he?" Solace asked, indicating Clive.

"The answer to your dreams, precious," Clive said, linking an arm through hers. "Let me buy you a grog."

In a flash, Solace slipped out of his grasp, twisted one of his arms behind his back, and had her lightsaber hilt nudged up against his chin.

"Did I mention Solace was a Jedi, too?" Ferus asked.

Solace released Clive, who smiled at her discomfort, and they all headed into the noisy cantina located near the spaceport. The music and conversation would cover their words.

Clive rubbed his hands together as he surveyed the mangy dive. "This is just about the most beautiful sight I've ever seen."

They ordered drinks and food, and Clive ate ravenously while Ferus filled the group in on what had happened to him. They told him about the attack on Solace and her followers. Ferus was grieved to discover that the Empire had acted so quickly and that the other Erased had been killed.

"The good news is that we all reactivated our information networks," Oryon said. "We were able to find out where the Imperial thugs were holding you."

"We're not ready for a real resistance

movement — not yet," Keets said. "But we can see a day where we could link up with other planets."

Ferus saw it, too. It was years away, he knew. But someday the pockets of resistance on each planet would communicate with each other and form a network. Maybe even an army. It all had to start somewhere.

Ferus nodded. "We just have to begin. And Coruscant is the perfect place to start. The Senate has always been full of informers, people eager for a bribe. Just because the Emperor has taken over doesn't mean it isn't still true."

"Yeah, we also heard Malorum is on Naboo on some top-secret mission he concocted for himself," Keets said. "So you don't have to worry about him for a while."

Naboo. A warning bell went off in Ferus's mind. Why?

Because Obi-Wan told me to be alert to any investigations into the death of Senator Amidala of Naboo. Her funeral had been held there, in the city of Theed.

He tried to dismiss the importance of Malorum's visit. There could be any number of reasons for him to go to Naboo. But he could not forget that Obi-Wan had told him that Malorum could threaten the future of the galaxy if he was allowed to continue his investigations.

For a moment, he felt a spurt of annoyance at Obi-Wan. The Jedi Master was sitting in exile, giving Ferus a vague order to watch out for something without telling him what was at risk. Ferus would have preferred a clear-cut mission.

Yet he couldn't ignore this.

He looked around at the table. He would go alone, of course. But he had the feeling that this unusual collection of fighters wouldn't let him. He wasn't sure how it had happened or why, but they shared a bond. Even Clive.

"I have to go to Naboo," Ferus said.

Keets put down the pitcher of grog he was about to pour. "Just when I was starting to relax," he moaned.

"I'm not asking you to come," Ferus said truthfully. "But I have to go."

He felt the weight of the moment as they considered his words.

Clive slammed down his heaping forkful of food. "This place has really gone downhill," he said. "Let's go."

CHAPTER THIRTEEN

Naboo was a lovely world. Theed was renowned across the galaxy for its natural marvels. The waterfalls kept the air in a state of constant, exhilarating freshness. Flowers and vines twined on every gracious building. The people of Naboo were known for their warmth and cordiality, their love of peace. There was an art to living, they felt, and their food, their buildings, and their clothes indicated this. It was a beautiful, ornate world, and Malorum wanted to blast it into space dust.

Everywhere he turned, he was met with smiles and bows. When he asked questions, he was met with earnest desires to help him, thoughtful frowns, fingers clicking on data keys, careful reviewing of records.

But no answers. "Alas and sadly . . ." the functionary would say with a helpless shrug.

It was infuriating. No one defied him, no one

refused him, but no one gave him what he wanted. As soon as he thought he had grasped something as firm as carbonite, he found he was holding only air. And there was no way he could threaten them, for they seemed to cooperate fully.

Why did he get the feeling that behind his back they were delighted to thwart him?

He could see why the Emperor decided to send an Imperial battalion here despite the objections of Queen Apailana. They hadn't interfered in the planet's governance, but their presence was a necessary reminder of who was actually in charge. They had completely taken over one of the gracious domed government buildings in Theed, right next to the vast hangar. It was a smart choice. They could monitor all official comings and goings, and also use the hangar to store explosive devices should the people rebel. Strictly against Senate rules, of course, but who would ever know?

Malorum thought that the citizens of Theed would have learned something from the Trade Federation blockade years ago. They'd discovered just how vulnerable they were. The fact that they had won that particular skirmish had been mere luck. If the Emperor had been in control they would have been cowed and defeated.

Naboo was completely reliant on the rest of the galaxy for its industrial materials. They had no factories to speak of. If Malorum had been in charge, Naboo would have attacked surrounding worlds that were rich in minerals and industry. But no — they just kept on making their clay pots and their paintings and their clothes and stupidly left themselves vulnerable.

Malorum walked by the Imperial garrison, hoping the sight of it would give him fresh energy. He had visited the place where Senator Amidala's body was prepared for burial. He received no new information . . . except a crash course he didn't need in the funeral rites of the Naboo. Apparently the grandmothers were designated as the ones who dressed the body and prepared it for the "last journey."

The fact of Padmé's death was recorded . . . but that was all. There was no hint of how she'd died, nothing for him to go on. Naboo customs precluded any questions about the possible father of her child; the family was given privacy. There was no doctor's report.

Malorum's steps slowed. How stupid. Of course, if the records did not show him what he wanted, he must go to the source. Padmé Amidala's grandmothers.

One problem was that the Naboo did not have a world directory. Citizens did not have to register with the government, something he knew that the Emperor would change as soon as he got around to it. Privacy was prized here. In addition, everybody seemed to know everybody else, through a network of clans and families. If you had to ask for an address, it was proof that you didn't know the person well enough to contact them.

A small problem. Not an insurmountable one.

Malorum crossed to the building that housed the Naboo Essentials Provider, a typically gentle name for the office that controlled the power grid. He paused just inside the door to examine a large holo-map on the wall, a graphic image of the main power generator. He noted the corridors lined with elec-tron gates, the catwalks, the bridges to dozens of levels, the deep central core. Impressive. The Naboo did have some technical expertise after all. This would be an excellent world to exploit.

He strode into the main office and demanded to see the manager. In the usual display of polite eva-sion he was told that the office was about to close, but if he'd come back tomorrow . . .

"I am a personal representative of Emperor Palpatine. Get him for me now," Malorum snapped. He couldn't wait to squeeze the information out of these maddening people like pulp from a muja fruit.

The clerk rushed into an inner office, ornate robes flowing. Malorum had been waiting, hoping for this. He strode after him. He pushed through the door, almost knocking the man to the floor.

The manager stood up from his desk, his mouth

gaping. He was older, his graying hair standing out in tufts over his ears. He had a kind face and gentle eyes. Malorum despised him immediately.

"I am looking for the addresses of the grandmothers of the former Senator Padmé Amidala."

"Senator Amidala, alas and sadly, is deceased."

"I am of course aware of that." Malorum slammed his hand down. "This *desk* is aware of that! I am the eyes and ears of the Emperor himself. Tell me the names of her grandmothers. I know you know them so don't waste my time with denials."

The man swallowed. He quickly consulted a hand-crafted ledger. "Winama Naberrie. Ryoo Thule."

"Give me their addresses."

"Winama Naberrie, alas and sadly, died before the Battle of Naboo."

"Then the other one!" Malorum roared at the man. He didn't like to lose his temper — he felt a loss of control was always a mistake, but he'd been provoked by hours of evasions. And it could be effective.

To his surprise, the man stood his ground. "Ah, well, I don't have that information per se, you see. This is the office of the Essentials Provider —"

Malorum had had enough of this. Always it was the same. The person would tell him he really didn't have the ability to help him while maintaining an expression of deep concern, then repeat his title or the name of the agency, and Malorum would be led round and round in a helpful, polite way that got him nowhere.

He put his blaster next to the man's cheek. "Do you see this?" No more yelling now. Just a quiet voice that held menace.

The man's expression turned to fear. "Yes."

Slowly he rotated the blaster until the barrel was pointing toward the outer office. "I am going to take this blaster and shoot everyone in this office in front of your eyes if you don't give me the information."

The man looked up at him. Incredulity turned to horror as he realized that Malorum was perfectly capable of doing it.

He bowed his head. "Ryoo Thule now lives in the lake district of Naboo in the family villa called Varykino. In Translucence Cove."

"That isn't much of an address." Malorum gave the blaster an extra push against his cheek.

The man raised his head. Something flashed there, some defiance that Malorum decided he didn't have time to smash. Naboo would come to understand, as all worlds would, who was in charge.

"That is the way we do things on Naboo. It is the only direction I can give you."

Malorum wanted to shoot him, but he stormed out instead.

He had what he needed. It was tedious to have to do his own investigating, but he couldn't trust anyone else. He had to dig and dig until he had what he wanted. He knew the lake district was remote; he'd need local transport. All to see an old woman who might hold the key to something he still didn't understand.

CHAPTER FOURTEEN

Solace and the others landed their ships on an entry platform on the outskirts of Theed. They knew the Imperials were monitoring the hangar. Clive was familiar with Theed and led them through the streets.

"The people of Naboo are no fans of the Empire," Clive told them. "They'll keep their mouths shut. Just follow me. I know Theed well."

"I don't need a tour of cantinas," Ferus told him suspiciously.

Clive laughed. "I can show you those, too, mate. But let's start with some contacts. I know a former captain in the army who can help us — Gregar Typho."

"I know him," Keets said. "I interviewed him a couple of times. Senator Amidala trusted him."

"Lead on," Ferus said.

Captain Typho was in an office off one of the

wide boulevards of Theed. He rose from his desk a bit awkwardly, in the way of an active man who was unused to office work. He had a small eye patch over one eye and was wearing a uniform over his powerful build. He remembered Keets well and greeted Clive warmly.

"I heard you were in prison," he said.

"I wasn't crazy about the accommodations. This is my friend, Ferus Olin. We're all here to help locate an Inquisitor named Malorum."

Captain Typho nodded. "We know he's here. We've been tracking his movements. He began at the Imperial battalion offices — we know they're setting up a spy network here. We're keeping them under surveillance even as they spy on us. They've taken over a government building next to the hangar. Despite the laws of Naboo, which forbid it, we suspect they are secretly stocking weapons and explosives there."

Curran Caladian frowned. "That's against the laws of the Senate as well. Do you think they're planning to take over the government?"

Typho nodded grimly. "It's possible. They have assault ships in orbit. They've done this with equally uncooperative worlds, under the guise of 'keeping order in the galaxy.'"

"I'm well aware of their tactics," Ferus said. "They did it on Belassa, where I come from."

"I've heard about that," Typho said. "It's what we fear. That's why we've been keeping a watchful eye on Malorum. We know how close he is to Emperor Palpatine. The curious thing is that he doesn't seem to be on official business. He checked in with the Imperial regent, of course, but after that, he's been on his own, keeping a low profile."

"So what has he been up to?" Keets asked.

"We've been receiving reports from government officials that he's been investigating the funeral of Senator Amidala."

His face darkened. "I too have investigated the Senator's death. I don't believe the official reports that the Jedi killed her. They were her friends. She believed in them absolutely; she never believed the rumors during the Clone Wars that they were abusing their power."

"I don't know why Malorum is interested," Ferus said. "I only know he must be stopped."

Typho nodded. "I'll do what I can to help you. What do you need?"

"Do you know where he is right now?" Ferus asked.

"He's no longer in Theed," Typho replied. "We just got word from the Director of Essentials, who said that Malorum forced him to reveal the whereabouts of Senator Amidala's maternal grandmother. We've been trying to contact her, but she lives in seclusion and hasn't answered our comm signals."

Ferus stood. "You'll have to direct us there. But first, I need to speak to Queen Apailana."

Ferus and the others were ushered into the Queen's presence in the throne room in the palace. She was wearing her ornate ceremonial robes — deep blue with a matching headdress. Her face was painted white, with a red slash on her upper lip, called the scar of remembrance. Captain Typho introduced each of them, and they all inclined their heads in a short bow. Typho then gave the queen a brief explanation of why they were on Naboo.

"I'm honored to meet so many distinguished guests," the Queen said in her soft voice. "I offer you welcome."

"Queen Apailana," Ferus said, bowing his head again. "I have come to ask you something I have no right to ask you."

"Yet here you are," Queen Apailana said.

"I request that on my signal, you shut down all comm systems on Naboo. Internal and external comm systems."

The Queen looked startled. "That is quite a large request," she said.

"Queen Apailana, the Jedi as we knew them are

no more," Ferus explained. "Jedi Master Solace and I are among the last left alive. You were once a friend of the Jedi and the Republic. Please trust us once more. Malorum is dangerous not only to Naboo but to a peaceful future for the galaxy. I know what I ask is difficult."

"I am reluctant," the Queen said slowly. "Yet you are right — our history with the Jedi has led me to trust what they say. I never believed the official story of Senator Amidala's death. I have encouraged Captain Typho to keep searching for answers, even though it seems there are none to be had. Near the end of her life, the Senator still had faith in the Jedi. We were in constant contact, so I am sure of this. I still think of the Jedi as friends — no matter if there is one or one thousand."

"Then you'll do it?"

"On two conditions," the Queen said. "One, that you send the signal only out of the most dire necessity."

"That of course would be the case," Ferus answered.

"Two, I will shut communications down for one hour only," Queen Apailana continued. "I cannot endanger the citizens of Naboo for longer than that. We can fake an outage for a time, but the Imperial presence will become suspicious if the outage lasts any longer."

Ferus inclined his head. "That should be all I need. Thank you."

"Thank you for your service," the Queen replied. Now it was her turn to incline her head in a gesture of respect to Ferus and the others. "Thank you for not giving up."

CHAPTER FIFTEEN

Ryoo Thule had been up before dawn. She had walked down to the lake to see the sunrise. She had noticed on the way to her home, as she climbed the steep grade back to the house, that she was out of breath. Yet she didn't feel winded, exactly.

She pressed a hand to her side, then against her heart. She was an elder now, but she was still surprised when her body told her so.

She remained robust and strong, still capable of walking the steep, winding paths of the cliffsides along the lake. She just had to learn to walk slowly, not scamper up the way she had when she was a child.

That must be it.

On those early morning walks her family strolled beside her. Not the family who still lived, her daughter Jobal, her son-in-law Ruwee, their child Sola and her children, her own namesake Ryoo and her sister Pooja. Not her sister and her children.

It was her husband, long dead, who walked beside her. Her good friend, Winama Naberrie (how they had plotted to marry off their children! How surprised they'd been when they'd actually fallen in love!) and her beloved grandchild, Padmé. In some ways Padmé felt closer to her now that she was gone.

From an early age Padmé had been on her way to somewhere else. Oh, she had been the most loving granddaughter possible, but her visits had been respites from a busy life. She'd never suggested, by word or look, that this was the case. Her whole heart had been in those visits. Ryoo had felt it just the same, because she was closer to Padmé than any of her other granddaughters.

She'd had her secrets. Ryoo knew that. She'd known before Padmé had that she was in love. She'd known that love was entwined with heartbreak.

Padmé's death had broken her own heart. Ryoo had, according to custom, been the overseer of her funeral. She had kissed her granddaughter's cold cheek. She had tucked small white blossoms into her clothing and hair. She had wept on a cold floor.

The grief was still a stone in her belly, but she'd

found peace here. Padmé had loved this place, and Padmé was all around her. Padmé was part of the galaxy now.

Part of her stays. Somewhere out there in the stars. I feel it. It is enough to feel it. Perhaps someday . . .

Ryoo stood at the window looking out at the azure lake. She pressed a hand to her chest and felt her heart flutter. Why had she woken this morning with such a sense of foreboding? Why did Padmé feel so especially close to her today?

What was this feeling? Why was she so restless?

She had been here for six months, mourning. It was time to return to her life in Theed. She wasn't too old to find a renewed sense of purpose. Padmé would want that.

Maybe that was the source of her anxiety. She knew it was time to let go of her grief, and she was reluctant. She had to remind herself that leaving this place wouldn't mean leaving her memories of Padmé behind.

Ryoo paused by the comlink station. Its insistent blinking told her of messages she should listen to. But she wasn't ready. Not now. Later. Her family was used to her returning messages later in the day. They wouldn't worry. They knew her grief needed solitude.

Ryoo smiled at that insistent red light. It spoke

of the warm voices of friends and family, eager to bring her news or check on her well-being. It contained the threads of her life.

It was time to pick them up again.

She would leave tomorrow. It was time.

She heard footsteps in the reception hall below. Strange. She was alone here, without servants, and the neighbors weren't close. She would have seen a gondola, or a speeder, if someone had come to visit.

She walked down the stairs, her slippers whispering on the stone.

He stood, his face in shadow. His robe was deep maroon, the color of dried blood. For a moment her steps faltered. It was as though Death himself had come to call.

Then she recognized the flutter she had felt all morning, the unease. It wasn't old age at all, it wasn't restlessness or the realization it was time to be gone.

It was fear.

Padmé, Padmé, I'm afraid.

She told herself she was being ridiculous. She'd been right; she'd been here too long alone. She walked forward, her hand outstretched, ready to greet the stranger, for on Naboo every stranger is a potential friend.

He threw back the hood. She saw his eyes, and suddenly she understood, with absolute certainty, what she'd felt the moment she'd awakened. She'd looked for the streaks of lavender that meant the sun was rising, light infiltrating darkness. Now she knew what had been chasing her throughout the day, what she'd believed, what she'd feared.

She was going to die today.

CHAPTER SIXTEEN

The old woman was still strong. At first she appeared to greet the stranger with respect. She even offered him tea, which he refused. Malorum hadn't received the title of Inquisitor for nothing. He knew when even the most skillful being was holding back.

No matter. He would find out. He had come to the end of his journey. He had no more time to waste.

"I know about Naboo rituals," he said. "I know that you were in charge of your granddaughter's funeral."

The woman, small and sturdy, her white hair coiled in back of her head, smiled in a condescending way that made Malorum's vision go red for a moment. "No one is 'in charge' in our funeral rites. I was there to support our grieving family. Naboo, you see, is not hierarchical like your system. Yes, we have a queen, but we elect her, as well as her advisors."

Malorum felt his teeth grind. "I don't need a lesson on Naboo political philosophy."

She inclined her head, but he could see its meaning. She thought him a pompous fool.

She would learn.

"The grandmother is there to make sure everything runs smoothly. This can be quite complicated in a state funeral," she continued.

"Senator Amidala died of what, would you say?"

"We don't know."

"Were there marks on her body?"

He saw her flinch. She pressed her lips together and shook her head.

"Who brought her to Theed?"

"I don't know. I was summoned after she'd arrived."

"She couldn't have come on her own," Malorum said dryly. "She was dead when she got here."

The grandmother's cheeks suddenly flushed with anger. She didn't like the casual way he spoke of her beloved granddaughter. Yet he was choosing his words with great care. The only way he would get anything out of this woman was to anger her.

"Whoever brought her to us did so with great care and gentleness, and that was all that concerned us at the time," she answered.

"She was pregnant."

Her lips pressed together.

"Did the family know who the father of her child was?"

"That is a private matter."

"Would you like to spend some time in an Imperial prison?"

"No, not really," the woman said. "But if you think threatening me with it will give you the answers you want, you're mistaken."

She looked at him. Her eyes were dark gray dusted with gold. Unusual eyes. He was almost mesmerized for a moment, seeing himself reflected in them, seeing all the contempt she felt. He got a sudden flash of what she was inside, what she was feeling.

Love. Great love.

Strength. Courage.

He pushed those irrelevancies aside and looked beneath.

Something she'd suspected, something only she suspected . . .

"Padmé did not share with us the father's name," she said. He could see perspiration around her hairline. She was nervous. "We didn't ask. Such things are private matters on Naboo. Because of the Clone Wars we hadn't seen her in several months. She was the light of our lives, and our sorrow and grief is more than you could possibly know. Why you think you have a right to come here and question me is beyond my understanding."

"I do have a right," Malorum said. "The Emperor has given me that right. I am his personal representative."

He was talking, but the words were too familiar, he had said them so many times. He was listening now. He was hearing what she was feeling, not what she was saying.

"Did you know Anakin Skywalker?" he suddenly barked.

"He was a friend of my granddaughter's," the old woman said.

"Did you ever suspect that he was the father of her unborn child?"

Something flashed in her eyes, not anger this time. Something . . . it was the key.

She knew something.

No . . . *suspected.*

He thought of the intuition inside him, what he thought of as his "river." It had always been there. When he was younger he believed he was just smarter than anybody else. Now he knew it wasn't intelligence, it was another sense, bigger than he was. His frustration was that he couldn't control it the way he wanted to.

But it was here now, and he could focus it on Ryoo Thule.

His gaze must have unnerved her, for she looked away. He felt something rise in her, some hope, something she was grasping even as she battled against his will. Something she did not want him to know, and would never betray.

The knowledge ripped through his brain like a rip in fabric, tearing away his misconceptions. He almost leaped with the exaltation of it. Only the most strict discipline, the habit of years of interrogations, kept him standing, with the same expressionless face.

The child was alive.

She had spoken of her granddaughter, but never of the child she carried. That she did not was in itself a signal.

"The child is alive," he said. He could see on her face that she believed it.

Now the questions came quickly as he advanced upon her, as she shrank before him.

"Have you ever seen the child?"

"Has anyone contacted you about the child?"

"Has anyone visited the child?"

"Did Padmé know the child was living before she died?"

"Did she give the child to someone?"

"Is someone hiding the child?"

"Where is the child?"

The questions kept coming. The old woman

threw up her hands as if to ward them off like blows.

When she regained control and lifted her face, it was filled with defiance. She knew little, he could see, and she would tell him nothing.

So he killed her.

CHAPTER SEVENTEEN

The beauty of the lake was astonishing. Varykino perfectly fitted into the landscape, turrets and domes rising from the rocks and water as they sped toward it, so close to the lake that their Naboo water craft, a gondola speeder, kicked up a wake.

Ferus barely noticed the deep jewel color of the lake, the arcing sky overhead. Before the gondola speeder had come to a halt he vaulted off it. He was filled with foreboding.

He and Solace left the others behind as they Force-leaped up the cliffs, finding toeholds and handholds while in midair. The others charged up the path.

The door to the graceful villa was wide open. He charged inside, his lightsaber held aloft.

Ryoo Thule lay crumpled on the stone floor. He leaned down and with great gentleness touched her cheek. It was warm.

Suddenly her eyes opened, giving him a shock. He'd thought she was dead. Her life force was almost extinguished.

Her eyes widened just slightly when she saw his lightsaber. He felt her fear dissolve and she looked at him with something like friendship. With that one glance he knew Padmé's family did not blame the Jedi for her death.

"He suspects," she whispered.

"Malorum?"

A nod. Then suddenly she seemed to gather strength. Strength enough to grab his tunic. "He can't tell anyone what he knows. You must protect . . ."

She lost her breath. Her fingers opened and she fell back.

"Protect what?" Ferus felt the urgency. He was lost in implication and mystery and everything he didn't know.

"For Padmé," she whispered. "For Padmé."

Life left her then.

He turned. Solace sat behind him on her haunches as easily as if on a chair.

"Want to tell me what's going on?" she asked.

Ferus looked at her helplessly. "I can't. I don't even know. I just know there's a secret that threatens the galaxy. Ryoo knew it, and now Malorum does, and we have to stop him. Obi-Wan Kenobi warned me."

She rose smoothly, quickly. She didn't need any more information. What he said was enough. "Kenobi? Then let's do it."

They ran out the door. The others were just hitting the top step.

"It's too late," Ferus said. "He's gone. But I think he's around here — we would have seen him take off."

"He must have hidden his craft," Oryon said.

"This flaming coastline is full of coves," Clive said. "But we should send the signal now!"

As soon as that was done, Ferus said, "Let's split up into twos. Malorum is a handful. Stay here, Trever."

"No."

Clive whistled. "It's so inspiring how he follows orders."

Ferus couldn't wait to straighten it out, so he took off alone. He knew Trever would follow, and he also knew the boy would stay undercover. His heartbeat drummed inside him with urgency. *The future of the galaxy is at stake,* Obi-Wan had said. *The secret can't get out.*

Luckily the communications were being jammed, so Malorum couldn't share his information.

Until the hour was up.

Ferus leaped to a spot on the steep side of the cliff, then jumped again. His boots landed in soft sand.

He heard the lapping of the blue water. The song of a bird. He felt the Force gather and now he could not only hear everything with crystal clarity but feel it as well, pulsating through him.

The Living Force was near. The dark side of the Force pulsed. He raced down the beach in that direction. A cluster of large rocks was scattered in the bay, and he Force-leaped onto the first, leap-frogging from one to the other until he was past the point of the land. Now he could see Malorum in a speeder gondola, ready to take off. Malorum looked over and saw him and the craft shot forward over the lake.

Ferus vaulted into the air and soared toward the craft. Malorum suddenly yanked on the steering mechanism, so the craft was headed straight toward him now at top speed. Ferus reacted as a Jedi. He did not retreat. He used the advance of his enemy to his own advantage.

He stopped his momentum in midair, waiting out the microsecond it took for Malorum to reach him. Then he somersaulted neatly over the craft. He used the updraft to power himself out of harm's way, then dropped onto the gondola.

Well — not dropped, exactly, in the neat way he could have accomplished even as an apprentice. Rather, he fell awkwardly, sprawling on the hull.

Sometimes the Force worked for him. Sometimes it didn't.

Malorum yanked the craft to the right, dipping it close to the water. Ferus flipped over, his feet skipping over the surface. At this speed, the water felt like permacrete.

"Ow," Ferus grunted through his teeth as the gondola bumped along and he hung on for his life. "Ow, ow, ow."

Using all his strength, he flipped himself back into the boat. This time he was able to access the Force with more precision, pivoting on his hands and delivering a well-placed kick to Malorum's chest. Malorum was knocked backward, loosening his grip on the controls. The gondola began to spin crazily. Ferus was almost thrown off the craft but reached out and grabbed on to the curved stern to steady himself. He reached for his lightsaber and activated it just as Malorum began to pepper him with blasterfire.

It was impossible for the Inquisitor to aim in these conditions, but he was doing a good job of trying. Ferus used the curved stern as a fulcrum, swinging around it as the gondola bounced, his lightsaber fending off the red and orange blaster streaks.

Off in the distance he saw the other gondolas approaching. Solace piloted one with Oryon hanging on grimly. Curran and Keets were in the other. Where were Trever and Clive?

Malorum pulled back the fabric of his robe on

one arm. Ferus felt the warning as propulsion. He leaped at his assailant. In midair he saw the gleam of the rocket launcher on Malorum's wrist. Malorum surprised him by rolling underneath him and then releasing the rocket.

Solace saw it before the others. She turned her gondola violently, shouting at Curran as she did so. He was too late. Unable to save the ship, he and Keets leaped into the water. The explosion sent shock waves across the lake.

And then Ferus saw Clive and Trever. *Of course*, he thought. The two thieves had stolen a boat.

It was a fast craft, sleek, with a chromium hull and a repulsorlift engine. Larger than the gondolas, it was still highly maneuverable and tremendously fast. Clive was piloting it straight at Ferus and Malorum.

The gondola was still moving at top speed, but without a pilot it swung in arcs and bounced on air currents and waves. Clive was heading straight for them, no doubt hoping to distract Malorum. It was a good plan. Ferus only hoped he didn't fall off before it happened.

Suddenly the air was alive with armored Imperial IPV-1 patrol craft. Malorum must have called them in before the Queen had been able to cut off communications.

The water around them exploded as the missiles

hit. The missiles were designed to intimidate. They couldn't risk hitting Malorum. But some of the patrol craft peeled off to attack the other gondolas and Clive and Trever's boat.

Ferus watched as one patroller dipped toward him. He leaped at Malorum, who shot his blaster at close range in Ferus's face. Ferus managed to deflect the blaster fire but Malorum dove toward a liquid cable that suddenly appeared above, higher than Ferus imagined he could. Malorum didn't bother to hook the cable, he just hung on as the IPV-1 took off higher, trailing Malorum behind.

Ferus leaped and managed to grab the tail end of the cable. In midair he saw the missiles heading for Clive's boat. Clive and Trever leaped off at the last possible second as their vessel was obliterated. At the same moment, two other patrol craft went after Curran and Keets, bobbing in the waves. The remaining Imperial pilots all turned toward Solace in the last gondola.

Ferus looked up into the muzzle of a repeating gun. He saw Malorum's fervid, triumphant face. He let go of the cable and dropped into the cold blue lake.

CHAPTER EIGHTEEN

Ferus plunged into the cold water as far down as he could to escape the fire above, inserting his Aquata breather into his mouth as he swam. He pushed forward in the direction he'd last seen Trever. He wasn't sure how good a swimmer the boy was, or if he could swim at all. He didn't know if Clive had a breather. Standard equipment for some, but not for others. Thanks to his Jedi training, Ferus was in the habit of having one on his utility belt, even if he was traveling to a desert world.

The water was so clear he should have been able to make out the others, but instead he saw nothing, just endless blue. Ferus fought against disorientation. He'd seen the others dive into the lake — where could they have gone? He swam farther down, feeling the pressure on his ears. He began to feel anxious. He couldn't abandon his friends, but he had to get back to Theed.

Suddenly he saw a strange sight — a shimmering transparent bubble heading toward him through the water. Was it some strange sea creature?

No — it was a ship. A ship shaped like a creature with a long tail. Inside he could just make out the shapes of beings.

Gungans.

Of course. Gungans ruled the underwater world of Naboo. From all he'd heard, they were friendly beings. Although they could wage a pretty nasty battle if they had to.

Just his type.

The strangely beautiful sub bobbed closer to him. The cockpit seemed to bend as it came closer, and Ferus stopped, motionless in the water, fanning his arms to keep himself in place. He felt no fear, only wonder.

A hand reached out through the cockpit bubble and somehow pulled him in. The rest of the group was crowded inside. Trever gave him a wan smile. Water streaming from his clothes, he dropped into a seat next to Solace.

"Nice rescue," he panted.

"Meesa welcome you to the bongo on behalf of all Gungans," their smiling pilot said. His friendly eyes twinkled at Ferus. "Good to stay underwater when the mackineek troopers are above."

"Where's Malorum?" Trever asked.

"He escaped," Ferus said. "I have no doubt he's on his way to Imperial headquarters at Theed. That's surely where he left his transport." He turned to their pilot. "We need your help."

"Meesa can take you anywhere you want —"

"No," Ferus interrupted. "All of you." He reached quickly for his comlink. After only a few seconds, he was put directly through to Queen Apailana. It was the only channel that had been left open.

"I need to call in another small favor," he said.

"You ask for much, Jedi Olin."

"You have no idea."

Now Trever had seen *everything*. He couldn't get over it. The underwater city had suddenly appeared, a series of huge bubbles like illuminated lamps. Inside were wide pathways with shadowy patterns and a murky green light.

And Gungans — he'd never even heard of them. He liked their friendliness and their loose-jointed strides. He felt safe in their underwater city. He would have liked to forget about everything happening above, but of course he was with Ferus-Wan, the owner of a one-track Jedi mind. Ferus asked to be taken immediately to their leader, explaining that he and Solace were Jedi.

Their rescuer, the pilot Yunabana, had been so

excited that he'd taken them directly to Boss Nass at a run.

Boss Nass resided in his own series of bubbles. While most of the Gungans were slender, Boss Nass was huge. His green skin had a grayish tinge, and Trever could tell he was an elder. He had three double chins and was wearing an elaborate coat the same color as his skin, so he resembled a giant greenish blob. He sat in a huge chair with waving fronds.

Now the Queen of Naboo was on holoprojector. The Naboo and the Gungans both felt that they owed the Jedi a great debt. They believed that the Jedi had been their only true friends during the Trade Federation blockade and had been responsible for helping them liberate their worlds. They readily agreed to a conference with Ferus.

Trever stood back with Clive, Keets, Curran, and Oryon as Solace and Ferus thanked Boss Nass and the Queen, and Boss Nass thanked the Jedi, and the Queen thanked Boss Nass, and Boss Nass thanked the Queen for what seemed a very long time, and finally everyone was silent.

"What is it that you want from us?" Queen Apailana finally asked.

"Wesa glad to help if help is needed," Boss

Nass said. He placed his hands on his belly and leaned back.

Ferus looked a bit nervous. He never looked nervous. Trever saw him swallow. It must be a big request.

"I need you both to use your security forces to attack and destroy the Imperial headquarters," he said.

Boss Nass jumped to his feet. "Yousa crazy?" he roared. "Attack Imperials? Maxi-bad strategy mesa friend! Yousa noticed they be controlink the wide-sea galaxy?"

Queen Apailana's tone was milder, but it was clear she was shocked as well. "Surely you realize the retribution that would be inflicted afterward upon both the Naboo and the Gungans. The Emperor would crush us. It would be swift and terrible, and many civilians would perish."

"That's for sure," Trever said under his breath. Ferus shot him a look that he didn't need a translator for. *Don't speak.*

"I understand the magnitude of what I ask," Ferus said.

"Why do you ask then?" Queen Apailana said.

"The future of the galaxy depends on it," Ferus said. "That I can promise you. The head of the Imperial Inquisitors, Malorum, has found out an important secret. If he is able to reveal it to the

Emperor it could destroy any hope we have of some-day living in peace and true justice."

"What is this secret?" the Queen asked.

"That I can't tell you. Yet you must trust me. We must strike this blow here, now."

There was a pause, so Ferus continued. "I have a way to avoid retribution. I would not propose this otherwise. I promise that no harm will come to your people."

"I'm listening," Queen Apailana said.

Boss Nass sat back. "Mesa, too."

Ferus turned back to Queen Apailana. "Your information network has reported that the Empire is illegally stockpiling destructive weapons in the Theed hangar in defiance of Senate regulations. If we blow up the weapons cache it would seem like a disaster the Empire had brought on itself. The officials back on Coruscant would wish to hush up the explosion so that the Senate wouldn't hear about it. The Emperor may despise the Senate, but he still needs it to cloak his crimes."

"Your plan depends on our winning the battle," Queen Apailana said.

"The combined might of the Naboo and Gungan warriors can defeat a battalion," Solace said. "They've gone up against far worse and won."

"I have the greatest confidence in the courage and daring of both your peoples," Ferus added.

Queen Apailana said nothing. Because of her elaborate makeup, Trever couldn't tell what she was thinking.

Suddenly Boss Nass lurched up, slapping the arms of his chair. "What a berry good trick, you say, Jedi! Get rid of Empire, protecting all our people, and no onesa ever thinkin' well of us! Bringsa out the fambaa anda power us up!"

They all turned to the holographic screen. The Queen's image was still impassive.

"Yes," she said slowly. "It is a berry good trick, as my friend Boss Nass says. And it might remove the Empire from Naboo for some time. If it works."

"Will you commit your forces?" Ferus asked. "We can draw up the battle plans here and coordinate when we reach Theed."

"Faster issa to goes underwater," Boss Nass said. "Wesa can bring the army thatta way."

"We'll be ready," Queen Apailana said.

CHAPTER NINETEEN

Ferus and the others waited aboard a Gungan military launching ship beneath the lake in Theed. Since the Trade Federation battle, the Gungans had designed troop transports, long and narrow, that could navigate the water caverns that networked below the surface of Naboo.

The transports lined up underneath the lake, their mineral skins tinted blue-green for camouflage. They waited for the signal from Captain Typho. Ferus exchanged a glance with Trever. He no longer bothered to order Trever to stay behind. It was a waste of breath.

Solace, Ferus, and Oryon would leave first. They were to head immediately to Imperial headquarters and break in. Ferus would split off and go for Malorum. Solace and Oryon would head off any attempt of Imperial officers to escape. Usually the higher up the officer, the more you could count on their having a separate escape route from the rest of the battalion.

Clive had begged off being included. "I'm a solo act," he told them. "Wars make me nervous."

Solace had snorted her disapproval.

The signal came. The Gungan ships rose slowly and then burst through the surface. Ramps slid out and connected with the land. Ferus, Solace, and Oryon raced off the ship.

The Naboo security force was already mobilizing in the streets, marching toward headquarters. Ferus could see several panicked stormtroopers racing to return to the building. Already ranks were forming lines on the building's wide steps. The first fire rang out from the front lines.

He would join the fight, but first he had to find Malorum.

They raced around the corner of Imperial headquarters and released liquid cables. It brought them up to the first bank of windows. Ferus had already networked with the Naboo and knew where the officers were located.

Solace paused. The sounds of battle had escalated. "May the Force be with you," she said.

Ferus nodded and took off through a window. He ran down the halls, which rang with confusion as officers scrambled to load data onto computers, no doubt following some sort of Empire protocol for a surprise attack. Others ran toward the back of the building where Ferus knew it connected with the Theed hangar.

That was where Malorum would be headed. He wouldn't stand and fight. He would cut and run.

Ferus increased his speed, mowing down stormtroopers that got in his way. The thud of his boots sounded out his purpose. He held his lightsaber aloft.

He burst through the grand double doors of the hangars. Amid the gleaming ships and stacks of cartons he saw the flicker of a red cape. Malorum had seen him and was running away. He chased him down a long hallway that connected to another grand building.

The hallway opened up into a gigantic circular area. Platforms and bridges were stacked hundreds of meters high. The space was filled with a low-level hum. He was in the Theed power generator.

The knowledge thudded through his brain. This was where the great Jedi Master, Qui-Gon Jinn, had fallen. Every Padawan had heard the story.

It was here, Ferus thought. *This is the place Obi-Wan fought Darth Maul to the death.*

But now it was different. He wasn't fighting a Sith. He was fighting an Imperial Inquisitor — skilled, with powerful weapons, yes. But not a Sith.

Then Malorum turned, baring his teeth in a smile. And showed Ferus his lightsaber.

CHAPTER TWENTY

Ferus was startled. He and Obi-Wan had both felt that Malorum was a Force-sensitive. But that was a long way from being proficient with a lightsaber.

Where had he received lightsaber training? Malorum held the lightsaber easily in a classic ready stance, the red shaft projecting downward.

Ferus circled him slowly, holding his dark gaze. So. A former Jedi and a Sith pretender were about to fight. Interesting.

Malorum charged. The two lightsabers clashed. Ferus felt a surprising amount of power from Malorum. Maybe this wouldn't be so easy.

But it would be done.

He whirled around in a one-hundred-eighty-degree turn, kicking out with his foot at the same moment. He missed Malorum's chin by a whisker.

Ferus liked to fight with his boots as well as his lightsaber. He had learned to fight without a lightsaber when he'd been a regular citizen of Bellassa. Sometimes that meant fighting dirty. Looking for openings, using whatever materials came to hand. He could still street-fight if he had to.

He fought without urgency just yet, circling Malorum, challenging him, watching him for weaknesses. Ferus ticked them off in his head. Malorum relied on agility but had little grace. He had strength but did not know how to use it effectively. But most of all — and this was what Ferus was sure would defeat him — Ferus could feel Malorum's emotion in his style. Anger fueled his attacks. It was a mistake many made. Not a Jedi.

After feints and attacks, they came to a long passage with curving walls. A series of energy gates ran down it. Electron rays pulsed in a rhythmic fashion. Ferus remembered this from the story he'd heard as a Padawan. The energy gates had slowed Obi-Wan and he'd been unable to come to his Master's aid in his final battle with Darth Maul. In those crucial seconds, he'd watched Qui-Gon receive the fatal blow and fall, right before his eyes.

Here he was in the middle of a battle, and he was suddenly pierced with a sharp sympathy for Obi-Wan. For the past weeks he'd been intimidated by the

Jedi Master, irritated by his silences, upset at his decisions. Now he fully realized how little he understood of what lay beneath.

I can't imagine what he's seen. How he's suffered. What he's lost.

He made it through the first energy gate but suddenly they buzzed shut behind and ahead of him. Malorum was in the next chamber. How odd it was to see your enemy and be unable to move.

He could just make out Malorum's words.

"You can't stop me," Malorum said. "You can only slow me down."

"Oh, I'll stop you," Ferus replied. "Even though I'll miss our conversations."

The energy gates sprang open. Ferus jumped forward, swinging his lightsaber. Malorum parried and came a little too close to connecting to Ferus's shoulder. He had to leap backward, and the energy gates shut again.

"I've learned from the best," Malorum grunted through his teeth.

"Siri Tachi. Obi-Wan Kenobi. Soara Antana. Yoda himself." Ferus didn't know if Malorum could hear him, but he felt the names of his teachers resonate inside him like a powerful chant. "You don't know what the best is."

The energy gates opened again and Ferus surged forward, driving Malorum backward. "Want to be a

Sith, Malorum?" he taunted. "Is that it? Palpatine's puppy is tired of biting ankles?"

Rage darkened Malorum's face. Good. Exactly what he'd hoped.

Malorum sprang forward in a fast combination that Ferus had a tough time parrying. The dark side of the Force hummed with him now as his anger grew.

Okay, maybe it was time for a new strategy.

Malorum reversed directions and was able to run out onto a catwalk. Ferus leaped to follow him. He wondered if Malorum was heading for an exit. He knew if Malorum was able to get out of here, he would lose him. It was almost as if Malorum knew the way and was leading him on. Maybe he was trying to lead him back to the Imperial army, hoping they were still fighting.

They fought furiously now, using every inch of catwalk. They fought around the deep central core, hundreds of meters down. Ferus used his advantage of Force agility to leap and somersault, giving power to his thrusts. He fought using the lightsaber only, saving another kick or an elbow for when he needed it, when Malorum wouldn't be looking for it.

He pushed Malorum back, forcing him to rely on balance to avoid falling into the pit below. Malorum twisted and turned, but he was beginning to sweat.

Ferus saw his chance. He left himself slightly

open, and Malorum charged. As he came in, Ferus slammed his elbow directly into Malorum's forehead. It stunned him for a split second, and Ferus used the hilt of his lightsaber to smash Malorum's lightsaber out of his hands. The lightsaber shot outward, directly over the pit.

Malorum's mouth opened in a cry that echoed off the walls. "No!" he shouted. Ferus could feel the Force pulsing as Malorum leaped into the air, straining to catch the lightsaber as it spun. Straining to harness the Force to push the lightsaber hilt toward him and carry him safely to the next catwalk.

Don't . . . strain . . . Ferus watched Malorum make the elemental mistake of any early-year Jedi student.

He saw that Malorum was blinded by need. If he lost the lightsaber, he would be disgraced. He would never be a Sith.

Malorum's lightsaber dropped like a stone. Still in midair, Malorum lost his grip on the Force. His cape flapped around him, and Ferus saw the panic in his eyes.

Then he dropped down, down, down, into the central core. And Obi-Wan's secret went with him.

CHAPTER TWENTY-ONE

The battle was over. Smoldering stormtroopers lay on the streets. Fallen officers were in the building where they'd taken refuge.

Captain Typho strode toward Ferus as he emerged from the Theed generator. "Your friends are all safe," he said, before Ferus could ask.

Ferus saw a blur of brown and blue, and Trever ran toward him, his blue hair flying, his tunic torn. "Did you get Malorum? Did you stop him?"

"He fell into the central core of the generator."

"So the secret is safe," Solace said, coming up to them. "Whatever it is."

"We'll clean up quickly," Captain Typho said. "There will be no trace of battle. We've been monitoring the comm system. Coruscant Imperial Control is trying to raise the battalion here but getting no response. They're sending a ship to investigate from a nearby system. It could be here within the hour. It's time to blow the weapons cache."

"Looks like we're up, mate," Clive said to Ferus. "It'll be a mite tricky, but I think I've got the explosives figured out so we can get out in time."

Ferus blinked at him. "You *think*?" he asked.

Clive grinned. "Your pal here helped me with a few ideas."

Ferus looked at Trever.

"Don't look at me that way," Trever said. "I'm not coming with you this time. Do you think I'm crazy?"

Clive and Ferus entered the great Theed hangar, empty now of all personnel. The area around the hangar had been cleared of people and any valuables, just in case the hangar blew up the surrounding area. Theed pilots had flown a few ships to safety, but they would have to sacrifice some of their fleet so that the blast wouldn't look suspicious.

"The trick is to arrange the stuff so that it blows here, in the center," Clive said. "The shock wave will go down, not out. But this side wall has to pack some explosive power so that it blows the Imperial headquarters, too. We have to account for the loss of those stormtroopers."

"Let's do it," Ferus said.

They approached the boxes cautiously. Clive began to open them with a vibro-cutter.

"Some of this is highly volatile baradium," Clive said, eyeing the instructions on the durasteel boxes. "Just don't drop anything."

"Right," Ferus muttered.

Carefully, they picked up the boxes and bins and moved them to the center of the hangar. They took the highly volatile synthetic explosive and pushed it against the wall. Then Clive carefully walked through, setting the sequence charges. "Trever fixed these so that they'll disintegrate with the blast — no trace of metal or explosive will remain. They'll never know we blew it."

"So how are we getting out in time?" Ferus asked.

"The pattern is designed so that one alpha charge will set off an explosion that will set off the next, and the next, and so on, until it gets so bloody hot in here that the whole place goes up. It's going to be one crazy blow," Clive said fondly.

"Clive? How are we getting out?" Ferus asked, enunciating each word.

"Oh. I have a plan." Clive placed the last alpha charge against a drum of missile fuel.

"Good," Ferus breathed in relief.

"We run." Clive placed the last charge down and set it. "Now!"

Ferus spurted after Clive, cursing him in his head. Clive was one of those insane individuals who enjoyed extreme danger. Ferus felt the first explosion at his back. He felt the heat on his neck. He charged toward the doors. The next explosion gave him a push at the small of his back that almost sent him sprawling. The third made the air come alive. He rode a wave of air out the double doors and landed on his knees on the street. Clive rolled over, laughing.

"Come on, it's not over yet," he shouted.

The Imperial headquarters blew as they raced under a pedestrian bridge. The bridge fell in a shower of mellow ochre stone. Ferus grabbed Clive and Force-leaped to safety.

Sprawled on their backs, they watched as half the hangar burned and Imperial headquarters collapsed in a heap of rubble and a giant cloud of dust.

Coughing, they made their way to Solace, Oryon, Keets, Curran, and Trever, who were standing with Captain Typho watching the awful spectacle.

"I'm sorry about the building," Ferus said. "It was a gracious part of Theed. It will take a long time to rebuild that hangar."

"It is a thing," Typho said. "The people of Naboo are more important."

CHAPTER TWENTY-TWO

The orbiting space platform in the Rainbow Nebulae was somewhere between Naboo and nowhere, and it was a good place to stop. The group refueled there. It had been imperative that they take off from Naboo immediately.

They all stood together while their ships were hooked up to the refueling stations. The sky above vibrated with red, orange, yellow, green, blue, and violet.

"I heard from Typho on the way," Ferus told the others. "The Empire is investigating, and it's already clear that they're going to engineer a coverup. There will be no retaliation on Naboo. And it appears that Malorum died in the explosion."

"Love it when a plan works like a well-timed chrono," Clive said.

There was a pause. It was time to say good-bye, but no one was sure who was going where.

Ferus was anxious to return to the roving asteroid base. There were things to do, systems to set up.
He needed to contact Obi-Wan and tell him that the
threat posed by Malorum was over.

"I have a safe place," he told the others.

"You only have to navigate through an atmospheric storm to get there," Trever amended.

"You are all welcome," Ferus said. "Each one of
you is now an outlaw from the Empire. You'll need
fresh text docs, a place to lie low."

Ferus looked at Solace. He was creating the base
for surviving Jedi. Solace had told him she wanted
no part of it. He hoped she would change her mind.

"All right, I'll come," she said gruffly. "But just to
check it out."

Oryon looked at Keets and Curran. "We've been
talking. As the Erased, we've hidden away for too
long. We want to return to Coruscant. But we would
welcome a place to be quiet and make plans."

"After this little adventure, I could use a rest,"
Clive said.

"You're going to come?" Solace asked disdain-
fully. "I thought you were a solo act."

"Must be your sparkling personality," Clive said.

Ferus's comlink signaled. That was strange.
There were only a few people in the galaxy with
access. He walked a few steps away from the others.
The message played, a miniature hologram.

He stared, listening, and ice entered his veins.

He walked back to the others and placed his comlink on his palm. He held it out. "I think you need to see this."

An image of Emperor Palpatine shimmered in the air. "Greetings, Master Olin, for I think you deserve that title. Times have changed, and you've changed with them. I think our departed Inquisitor Malorum was a bit too hard on you. On behalf of the Empire, I'd like to offer you amnesty."

"Hey, what about me?" Clive demanded of the message.

"And I'm issuing you an invitation," Palpatine's message continued. "Come visit me on Coruscant. I give you my personal word that you will have safe passage. Let us speak together, and if what I offer doesn't interest you, you may take your amnesty and go. This offer stands for twenty-four hours from the receipt of this message. I hope to see you soon. We have much to discuss. Until then, farewell."

The hologram faded.

Ferus looked at his friends. "So," he said, "what should we do? Accept a date with the Emperor?"